A POCKETFUL OF PIXIES

BETTINA M. JOHNSON

AQUA RAVEN PUBLISHING

A Pocketful of Pixies

ISBN: 979-8-9850697-2-3 (paperback)

Cover art by Tina Adams

PROLOGUE

I've been watching them for days now.

    They have no clue.

How delightful it is to know I have something they need yet will never have. How utterly delicious. I think I shall make a game of it. Not that I haven't been doing just so all along. But here in The Big Easy, it's time to pick up the pace. Shake things up a little.

Watch them scramble and search for answers.

Watch as the confusion has them erroneously guessing.

Watch as my toxic magic taints the little ones, causing them to revolt.

Watch as the suspicion begins to fester and boil, as they begin to take sides and wonder who among them is a traitor. For one of them is. And won't that be amusing to watch the fallout? All this planning coming to a head here where it all began...for me anyway.

Then I shall sit back and watch it all fall apart. The dynasty. The Fortune's fortune. And the irony is they will never know the reason why—nor who—brought them to total destruction.

I certainly won't tell them.

They will never know it was me all along—the betrayer among them. Causing just enough destruction that they will never find the answers they seek...or the cure for their friendly little ghost. Their Ellie.

I will be there to offer comfort and strength in their time of sadness as she fades into oblivion.

I will always be there...among the group.

One of the team.

The most important part. After all, I hold them all together and give them purpose, right? But after this week, nothing will matter any longer. They will be at my mercy.

And they will know my name.

I am Ruin.

CHAPTER 1

"*Y*ou show up late, complain about our lack of motivation, then get in a snit when we inform you of our little situation. And by little, I mean pixie-sized! You need to back off, Maggie Fortune, before I turn you into a mole."

Well, that wasn't what I expected from my younger and out of this world sister, Ellie.

By out of this world, I mean that quite literally—out—way out. Ellie is a ghost.

"And just how do you propose doing that? Your witchy magic doesn't work here anymore, Spooky."

Ellie gave me a death glare and swirled across the hotel room where she proceeded to hover over a chair, arms crossed like she intended to sit and ignore me. Only Elle can't likely as well sit being ectoplasm and all.

The rest of my crew were lounging around the room in various states of undress. Nothing nefarious was going on...we had rented an old home near the French Quarter on Esplanade Avenue for this lengthy stop in New Orleans, and it was unusually hot for late March. Therefore, clothing was coming off faster than a trucker's in a brothel.

"Ellie. Do you remember the summer we spent visiting Cousin Gertrude?"

Ellie made like she wasn't going to answer but then she sighed...loudly.

"Yes."

"Do you remember what you did that summer?"

"I'm not quite sure what you mean."

"Oh, I think you do. That's the summer you let all the ants out of Cousin Louise's ant farm, and they scurried all over her room and home and Cousin Gertrude never did find them all—even after she used magic to round them up. Do you remember how defensive you got and started huffing and puffing and blaming everyone for any infraction that came up to take the heat off a very guilty you?"

"I vaguely recall some kind of brouhaha," sniffed Ellie.

"Yes, well, you are doing the same thing right now. You are barking at me for being a few days late and stressed about rampaging pixies when we very well know it was you and that lousy Pandora chick who set them loose in the first place!" I shouted.

"Pandora is a fearsome crossroads demon who can run circles around you and your puny magic, so don't get all haughty and impugn her good name!" cried Ellie.

Good name? Is she serious?

"You do know she could take her magic and make mincemeat out of us? That wretched demon is a menace, and I'm surprised you're so enamored of her, Ellie. It's not like she is mentally stable or anything," drawled Nathara, who had the most amount of missing clothing. That she was draped across the sofa dangerously close to giving my boyfriend a free peek at her assets notwithstanding, at least she agreed at the menace that was one Pandora, crossroads demon and friend of my cousin Lily Sweet in Georgia. Dorie showed up and got up to no good with Ellie right before we'd left Texas, and I suspect the two were responsible for our pixie problem.

And oh boy, did we have a pixie problem.

They were currently running amok on the streets of the French Quarter, and we were certain they were the ones who'd inadvertently brought them to The Big Easy. New Orleans was flush with pixies who were mischievous troublemakers on a good day. Right now? They were causing so much turmoil, The Order of Origin had to be called in to shed light on how we were to clean up this mess and not involve the populace.

The paranormal denizens of New Orleans were not enthused, and everyone was blaming my troupe of paranormal monster-hunters. OK...so we were supposed to be here for an antique fair, but monster-hunting was our real calling...and secret profession. Therefore, my supervisor, Delvin Fitzwick, followed me to New Orleans after our little rendezvous in Sweet Briar, Georgia, and the ridiculous trumped-up charges against Lily. Thankfully, Lily Sweet was one crafty witch and managed to clear her name with help from family and friends, and yet another psychotic witch is behind bars. We seem to have our fair share of nutty witches causing bedlam, and I for one am over it!

"We didn't do this! We didn't!" Ellie protested, looking at everyone in the room in turn. "We just took Chuck and two of his friends away from Sweet Briar, Georgia because they wanted a ride in the RV. Remember when we left Texas? We turned them loose in Serena and Sydney's RV, but that's it. Pandora left, taking Chuck and his buddies back with her once they were discovered. I don't know where *these* pixies came from!"

"Have you nabbed any of them? Do they know Chuck? How does one converse with a pixie anyway?" I asked.

"Very carefully," stated Daracha. Madame Myna, her side-kick, glowing softly from her crystal ball nearby nodded in agreement.

"That goes without saying, Dara, but I'm still wondering just how much those critters understand. I mean Chuck is positively loquacious compared to most pixies...and I think it means he's been...well...altered."

"Do you think he's been magically enhanced?" asked Bella, an earth elemental with youthful exuberance, despite the fact that she is probably older than all of us combined. Yet to most folks, she appears as a gum-popping teenager with attitude to spare.

"Could be. I've spent so much time lately doing research, it seems like something has been done to Chuck and maybe the others to make them have drastically distorted personalities. Now, as for lack of motivation, I did not suggest any such thing, despite what Ellie says." I glared at my recalcitrant sister who continued to sulk. "I only commented my surprise that we hadn't yet set up in Fairgrounds. And did anyone check to make sure the shuttle service knows where we're staying and can get us to and from the French Quarter in timely fashion?"

While we were staying in the French Quarter, the main antique troupe—those non-magical and running my father's end of the antiques and appraisals business—were sequestered in the Fairgrounds neighborhood at the race-track where New Orleans held several fairs and the Jazz Festival every year. Our RVs were parked there, and I was already regretting my decision to stay so far from the action.

What if the shuttle service couldn't get us to our jobs in time to open every day? We only had one car to share this time around.

What if the main crew needed me on hand to supervise set up and put out any fires?

What if Bob, my rather large and uber-lazy tuxedo cat suddenly felt he need to tear up a centuries-old tapestry hanging on the wall in the living room?

"Bob! Get away from that and behave. You are lucky the rental company made an allowance and let you stay here with us. Otherwise, you'd be living in Estelle's cramped quarters for the duration of this trip!"

Estelle Longo ran the daily operations for the Antiques and Mystic Uniques Caravan, our traveling antiques appraisals business. I left the caravan in the capable hands of my father's trusted human manager. Her two assistants, Sandy and Cassie Booker, usually dealt with our human workers and any questions and issues that came up. I ran the paranormal side of the show with everyone present, a great cover for what our true profession entailed.

You see, my small group of misfits, which encompassed several different Breed—what we call ourselves to differentiate between our human counterparts—hunted monsters in our spare time.

We had vampires, shifters, elementals, witches—just to name a few, and we all kept on the lookout for malevolent paranormal activity in every town we visited. You'd be surprised to realize just how much nefarious ne'er-do-wells actually mingled with humans on a daily basis, causing chaos wherever they went.

As head of the US Division of The Order of Origin...or just the Order...the law in the paranormal world, it was my job to keep my group working hard to eradicate any threats to the human and peace-loving paranormal populace. Long strides have been achieved in the last several decades, which eliminated the more immoral-leaning paranormals, and peace has reigned...in a manner of speaking. We always seemed to have a renegade witch, vampire, or even a few demons who couldn't let go of the old ways and preyed upon those less powerful.

That's when we stepped in and changed their minds...or ended their lives.

Business has been brisk as of late!

"Why are you doing research?" asked Bella.

"Because of what happened in Georgia to my cousin, Lily. Accusations flying left and right about her being a dangerous dark witch, and the law is messed up. I not only supervise our small group, but I handle the US end of the Order," I explained. "I find I am sorely lacking in knowledge of other Breed and lore and traditions. And that can't be—not anymore."

"That's because you're a witch. Witches only educate on witchy things. You people have a superiority complex—which is your downfall." This was from Nathara. She was a dark witch herself, but I'd recently discovered she was also a shifter—something she kept concealed from the rest of the group. She must have realized what she'd just said, because she quickly covered her faux pas with an explanation. "Unlike *my* family. Even though we are dark witches, we became highly familiar with all the Breed."

We had a prickly relationship to say the least. Sometimes I thought we'd turned a corner and moved past her animosity toward yours truly, but then Nathara would do or say something, and I came to realize we might never be friendly. Oil and water and all that jazz.

"Anyway," I said, ignoring Nathara, "I'd like to know if Chuck is involved in any way which would mean that Pandora chick has something to do with this."

I heard a collective hiss from Bella, Sydney, and Serena. Forget for a minute the twins are succubae and therefore demons right along there with Pandora, a friend of Lily's, and a menace in a miniskirt. For some reason undisclosed to me, the three women hated her with a vengeance.

"That Pandora chick is a crossroads demon, therefore she is a scourge! She must be behind this chaos. I say we hunt her down and turn her into a pile of ash," growled Serena.

"I agree," snapped Sydney, with Bella nodding her agreement.

"I'd like to see you try," purred Nathara, earning scowls from all three.

"You think we can't take her?" asked Bella.

"I vaguely remember everyone present being frozen in time then awakening to all manner of undress and disarray. I'd say Pandora is the strongest among us and not one to be trifled with." This from Dara, who didn't seem to have an opinion on the crossroads demon one way or another.

"She's not one of us nor will she ever be!" barked Sydney.

"Well, if she did this—behind my back, mind you—she most certainly will be among us. I don't know anyone who can control the little beasties better than Dorie," cried Ellie.

A collective groan sounded around the room. It seems Pandora wasn't popular in this crowd. The men certainly ogled the leggy blonde, but as far as personality, hers was over the top chaotic on a good day. I shudder to think what spending any more time with her than necessary would be like and wondered how Lily did it.

"Call her, Ellie. You have her number. Find out if this is some kind of elaborate prank on her part then tell her to get down here and fix it. It's not like time and space are an issue for someone like her," stated Antoine. "Pandora can be here in seconds if necessary."

Antoine was my trusted second in command and a vampire. Tall, dark, and handsome with ice-blue eyes that seemed to see and comprehend all, Antoine was the silent, imposing type who kept to the shadows—vampire status notwithstanding. Antoine hated being in the spotlight.

He'd been out of sorts lately, but unable or unwilling to tell me what was bothering him to the extent he was even more aloof than normal. I knew he wasn't particularly fond of New Orleans or being down here. Apparently, Antoine had too many relatives roaming these parts, many who chose to operate slightly on the wrong side of the law...and his name, and that of his family, proceeded him.

"I will do just that!" cried Ellie. "You'll see. Dorie didn't have anything to do with this mess. You can bet on it."

CHAPTER 2

*I*f I was a betting sort of person (I'm not), and I had to choose whether or not Pandora caused all the problems currently haunting the French Quarter, I'd bet on her being the puppet master to these pesky pixies. And I think I'd win that bet.

Oh, she denied everything of course. Even offered to come down and sniff out the source of our woes, but I managed to convince her to remain in Sweet Briar, Georgia and far away from the group. I didn't need that kind of tension and turmoil in my life right now.

Nobody did.

Pandora also informed us that Chuck was safely at home, tucked away in his tiny house with the rest of his buddies...so the ones we were dealing with down here seemed to have no connection to the ones in Georgia. I hoped anyway. I didn't trust Pandora any further than I could toss her...and seeing as I was sure I'd never be able to get close enough to try? Yeah.

"Where is our crew set up?" Dara asked.

"We are on the right side of the fairgrounds near the grandstands now that the racing season is over. Right off

11

Gentilly Ave. and the main entrance. Our RVs are parked in the far right corner once you enter, but we are set up right on the greens near the entrance," I replied. "In the center of the track."

"Boulevard," said Antoine.

"Come again?"

"Gentilly Boulevard. You said avenue."

"Oh. Well. Yes. Boulevard then. I'm sorry." I gave Antoine a shrug. "I can't remember all the names of the places we visit."

"Understandable. But considering this is where I grew up, it would be difficult for me not to remember."

"Of course! I hadn't forgotten. Did you grow up close the Fairgrounds neighborhood then?"

"My family lives around here, yes. We like the proximity."

"To the fairgrounds?" I asked.

"The cemetery."

"Ah. Um. Yes."

St. Louis Cemetery #3 and the others bearing the same name but spread around the city, the vast mausoleum-filled final resting ground of some of New Orleans dignitaries and notorious citizens—voodoo queen, Marie Laveau among them—would be attractive to vampires.

"Hm, yes. My mother still lives in the family home on Moss Street, not far from the Spanish Custom House. She still attends Our Lady of the Rosary on Sundays and takes in the races on the weekends during the season."

"Your...mother? Will we...I mean...I didn't realize, um...do you want to visit her while we are here?"

"No."

"No?"

"No."

The woman must be over five hundred years old if what I knew of Antoine was accurate. The mind boggled. That

Antoine was so reticent about visiting her while we were so close spoke volumes, and I wondered at the story behind it. But I also knew I'd respect the boundaries and walls he so obviously put up and not inquire further.

"So, you grew up in Fairgrounds?"

"Not the Fairgrounds neighborhood, just south. Bayou St. John. And I wouldn't say 'grew up,' New Orleans didn't exist when I was born. Although we were here when it was founded. Before actually, back when it was called Bulbancha. I have Atakapa-Ishak people in my lineage."

I blush slightly at my oversight. I assumed, just because Antoine was mostly of African descent, that he'd trace his lineage to some far-off African tribe. It didn't dawn on me that he'd have Native American or any other group mixed in. Although, why it should surprise me was odd considering his ice-blue eyes and my own Scottish roots blended with my mother's Romani blood and who knows what else.

"My people were never slaves, Maggie," Antoine continued as if reading my mind. "My father came over as a sailor on Columbus's second voyage and decided to leave Hispaniola on his own, then made his way to this region where he met my mother. She was the youngest daughter of the tribal elder. He became smitten with her and the rest, as they say, was history."

"Was he already a vampire? I mean...you don't have to answer me if I'm getting too personal, but how...?"

"How is it I am one? My father had African, Romanian, and Norse blood...and was very much a vampire. My mother was turned by him."

Well, that explains much...or not. And Romanian, like me. Interesting.

"And you came along born a full vampire then," I stated.

"In the year 528."

Eek.

. . .

"WE LIVED HERE A WHILE, but not as long as you would think. While this area is predominantly African, it wasn't always."

There are so many neighborhoods and enclaves that make up Orleans Parish, which encompassed all of New Orleans and the surrounding areas, it was sometimes a hectic and scattered attempt at keeping it all straight in my mind. But I adored all the many colorful and eclectic places that made up The Big Easy. Therefore, this pixie problem and the thought we might be responsible for allowing bedlam to run freely throughout the area rankled. I changed the topic back to that one.

"And now there are pixies everywhere, and if we don't do something about them, they will become the predominant fixtures around here," I stated glumly.

"So far, the outbreak has been closer to the French Quarter, with a few random events happening out here by the racetrack. That's what has me concerned this has something to do with Ellie and her friend," sighed Antoine.

"I don't know why Ellie is so enamored of Pandora. She is way too over the top in my opinion."

"Maggie, anyone who even hints at being an extrovert is over the top for you," he chuckled. Antoine was right. I'm the introvert of the family, and my sister Ellie is the life of the party. Always has been. Always will be.

"Where are we heading now?" I asked. Antoine, Dara, and I left the rest of the gang and were heading down Esplanade Avenue toward the French Quarter, but Antoine had just turned right onto Rampart Street.

"Louis Armstrong Park, or more specifically, Congo Square in the Tremé Lafitte neighborhood."

"Congo Square? That is quite the historic place, Antoine, no? Why are we going there?" asked Dara, shrewdly.

"For that very reason. An associate of mine knows someone who runs a local weekend market there who has information relating to the pixie issue. Cole has information for us and an offer. I am intrigued enough to go find out what his take is on all this."

Antoine went on to give us a brief history, explaining that in the 18th century, the colonial era for Louisiana's French and Spanish, the African slaves were usually allowed Sundays off, yet there were no laws allowing them to congregate. Despite constant threat of repercussions on these congregations, they often gathered anywhere they could find respite. Congo Square became one such place. It's a place where the enslaved would gather to sing, dance, play music, and even trade items at market.

The gatherings continued after the city became part of the United States with the Louisiana Purchase. It wasn't only the Africans that gathered—the native tribes would trade there, adding their music. Antoine's Atakapa-Ishak were one such group.

Visitors and townsfolk alike would gather around the square on Sunday afternoons after church let out to watch the lively dancing. But another practice soon took hold, that of performing voodoo acts for such audiences. Not the heavily secretive and religious kind that is traditionally kept from prying eyes and unwanted sources, but the kind left best to entertain tourists that is done today all over the city. It wasn't the most noted recreational activity in Congo Square, but even the voodoo queen herself, Marie Laveau, was known to perform there in the 1830s. Marie led voodoo dances in Congo Square but left her darker rituals for the banks of Lake Pontchartrain and St. John's Bayou.

. . .

IN THE LATE 19TH CENTURY, the square continued its tradition as a famous musical venue, this time for a series of concerts by orchestras of the area's Creole community. Congo Square came to be considered the birthplace of the culture and music of New Orleans, jazz and the sound one comes to expect when visiting New Orleans. In the 1960s, after a heated debate over what to do with the land surrounding the square, the city turned it into Louis Armstrong Park, which incorporates old Congo Square.

"Today the New Orleans Jazz Festival has events there as well as cultural and historic celebrations. They have an annual Red Dress run which starts there, and all the proceeds go to charity. And it's a gathering place for Martin Luther King Day. We are meeting Cole at the abandoned building adjacent to the square," said Antoine, upon completing his short history lesson.

"Abandoned?" I asked, my nose twitching.

"The building is a glorious piece of art in itself. It used to be, well...still is...the municipal building for the city that fell into ruin after Katrina. Now it is a much-maligned place where vandals—mostly kids—and homeless are damaging it bit by bit. No one can figure out what to do with it, and the funds from FEMA never came through."

"Why am I not surprised?" grumbled Dara.

"Indeed. It's a shame because many of the Mardi Gras krewes would hold their balls there during the season."

Turning right on St. Peter, then heading into the parking lot behind the aforementioned building, I noted the lack of life, the obvious signs of abandonment, and I became glum. Such a grand, old building would be a boon for the community, and I hoped something could be done to bring it back to its former glory. Just think of the benefits to the people living in Tremé Lafitte!

"Is Cole a big bad vampire such as yourself?" asked Dara teasingly.

"Worse." Antoine smiled down at our druid, patting her curly, chestnut hair in one graceful movement.

"What's worse than a scary vampire?" chuckled Dara.

"Cole is a siren."

"Oh, well, that's..."

Wait. A what?

"A siren?" I all but squeaked.

"Yes. A siren," said Antoine with a twinkle in his eye. "And some other stuff mixed in there. But he is indeed a siren."

Yep. Definitely scarier than a vampire in my book!

CHAPTER 3

I'd recently learned siren lore due to my involvement with cousin Lily's situation and her friend Tarni Vanderzee, herself being one. At first, I was yet again, clueless as to the origin of the Breed, assuming erroneously they had something to do with mermaids. While they did have something to do with mermaids, or merrow, they were their own unique Breed, something along the lines of paranormals descended from raven-like bird creatures. How they got their legendary siren voices was an intriguing tale that involved wars, strife, secrecy, and sadness. The merrow and sirens have been entwined in similar lore ever since.

Hunted relentlessly by the Order, sirens were rare. Those that had been nullified of power were left alone. But stories of their abilities were abundant...they were legend. Dangerous, enticing, breathtaking, and deadly. Strong. Stronger than any vampire, with the power to convince the most heinous acts. Sirens could tempt a mother to murder her children or convince a guard to press the button that would start nuclear war.

Yes. *That* dangerous.

How had Cole slipped through the cracks? Was he neutralized? His powers dulled?

The fact that my education was lacking—despite my rabid studying as of late—yet I was still appointed head of the Order's secret division here in the States, which rankled me more than I'd like to admit. It left a bad taste in my mouth and had me wondering why the upper echelon considered me a good choice. It couldn't be because my Aunt Morwena was a past leader, nor could it be due to my powerful and wealthy father and his connections...could it? It was a sobering thought, and I knew I'd have to make a phone call to my aunt soon, if not point blank ask my superiors why they chose me.

When I'd voiced my concerns regarding my lack of Breed knowledge to Delvin Fitzwick, the man directly above me in rank, and head of the Scottish division of The Order of Origin, he assured me I was concerned over nothing. I was a stellar leader of my group, and didn't our success in the field belie his appointing me so? We *were* a terrific group of monster-hunters, of that there was no doubt, but I had to wonder if my lack of Breed knowledge would someday come back to bite me on my posterior?

Coming around the side of the vast limestone-encased municipal building that led to Congo Square, I was thrilled to see small booths set up with folks selling their wares and a healthy number of people purchasing them.

This was more like it!

Music was playing from some unknown source—a common occurrence in New Orleans neighborhoods—and it gave some pep to my step.

"Wait here, ladies. Let me see if I can spot Cole."

Antoine took off back toward the building, leaving Dara

and me alone to wander among the booths, admiring the abundance of handmade goods.

"There is a veritable treasure trove of historical folk art pieces here, Maggie! Look at this!" Dara held up a replica mask that looked like those made by Ndaaka artists from the Ituri Rainforest in the Democratic Republic of the Congo, some of the art one could readily find in New Orleans if they knew to look for it.

I had on my gloves, so I picked up one of the masks to examine it closer. My reasons for wearing gloves are twofold. One, I handle quite rare and sometimes extremely delicate and expensive items that oils from my fingers could tarnish. Two, I am not only a witch, I'm also a psychic. Most of the Fortune side of the family has psychic ability and are witches. More specifically, I have psychoscopic and retrocognitive abilities. If I touch an item I am appraising with my bare hands, I can tell past ownership and provenance of said item. I get impressions and "hits" from all those who held the piece before me. My retrocognitive talent goes one step further. Sometimes, but not every time, when I touch an item, I get whisked back in time and can "see" events that transpired around the piece. I'm not really there, but I have a memory of events that play all around me.

It's kind of like virtual reality. A neat trick, but sometimes it lets me see things I'd rather not, and I erred on the side of caution. These items were newly made to look ancient, but I still rarely ever shook hands or held items without my trusty gloves. I wasn't even in the habit of touching loved ones...that is, until my latest occurrence—I began dating Tor.

Tor is the newest member of our troupe and I'd recently discovered he and I are on equal footing as far as The Order of Origin is concerned. He's some kind of super-secret spy for them. To this day, and despite officially dating now for a few months, Tor still made my heart do weird little flips every time I sensed him coming near. His full name is Torquil MacDonald, and he is a Scot, like me. He happens to be a sorcerer and half vampire.

Tor is tall, although more on the average side. He is lithe and makes one think of Highlander—kilts, and haggis—but in a good way. Or a swashbuckler. Or a... *yeah.* He has hazel eyes and reddish-brown hair that he wears longish and tied back. He also seems to have a perpetual five o'clock shadow that I find ever-so-disturbingly sexy.

"These are darling! And look at those sweetgrass baskets. You usually find them in the Carolinas, but these are just as lovely." I wiped my brow and sighed. The mugginess was making me sleepy, despite the lively music.

"Charleston...and the surrounding areas. Remember when we were there a few months back? That crazy drunken djinn," harumphed Dara.

"I hope Barney is doing well and hasn't fallen off the wagon."

"I heard Sydney tell Nathara that he'd told her he would let a few months pass by then prostrate himself in front of our dark witch and offer his hand in marriage, so smitten was he!"

"What? But...he promised to remain secluded—and free mind you—in the coastal marsh and leave everyone in peace! We can't have..."

"April Fool!" laughed Dara. She clutched her bag with Madame Myna hidden inside, to her chest, rocking with mirth.

"Oh! Hey, it *is* April first. You got me. Whew! I'm glad it was a prank on your part. The last thing we need is a lovesick genie hounding us," I exclaimed.

"Hmm, yes. Although I dare say it would have been amusing watching how Nathara handled the situation," snickered Dara.

We wove our way around the circle, taking in all the offerings at each booth for another five minutes until I happened to look up and notice Antoine heading in our direction with another man. To say the siren lived up to the hype was an understatement. Black hair, brooding dark brown eyes, and the body of a swimmer, Cole was lean and angular and reminded me a bit of old-time actor Gregory Peck...only prettier, if that were possible. They remained on the edge of Congo Square under the entrance portico of the municipal building. The humidity of the day already making my neck damp, I appreciated getting out of the sun for a bit. Dara and I joined the men with introductions all around.

Positioning ourselves under the cover of the entry portico and away from prying ears, I assumed we'd get down to business, and Dara and I would learn why Antoine wanted us to meet the attractive siren.

But first, we had another deferral to that conversation. One that had Cole confronting me in a most disturbingly antagonistic way.

"Maggie Fortune? The Maggie Fortune who is hunting sirens all over the place last I heard?" Cole asked, casting a suspicious eye in my direction.

"Hunting? I haven't...well, I mean..."

"Maggie doesn't hunt sirens, young man!" Dara sniffed, giving Cole the once-over.

"Yet I have it from a good source you were just in Sweet Briar, Georgia on the lookout for Tarni Vanderzee and her sweet briar witch status but didn't manage to find her. Going after your own cousin in due course instead. I don't know how I feel about this, Antoine. Tarni is my friend."

"You know her? Do you know where she is?" I asked, suddenly alert with this news.

"Like I'd tell you."

"You misunderstand. Delvin and the Order might want to

bring Tarni in under whatever trumped-up charges they have on her...but I promised my cousin Lily Sweet, that I'd let her know if I discovered Tarni's whereabouts so she could be warned."

"And why would a puppet of the Order aid a renegade siren? A dark witch? She is wanted you know...those trumped-up charges are rather severe."

"Because I owe Lily. Because I'm family...and I've heard some things from those who are close to Tarni."

"Were. Were close to Tarni. She isn't close to anyone, nor has she been for twenty or so years."

We eyed each other with hostility for a few minutes until Cole sighed, rubbing his hand behind his neck in frustration.

"But I don't have time for that now," he finally said. And if Antoine trusts you enough to have you lead him around on monster-hunting expeditions, who am I to argue? Just don't betray Tarni, Maggie Fortune. There are powerful people with a vested interest in keeping her safe and out of the clutches of the Order. You'd do well to heed my warning."

Was he threatening me?

I bristled and opened my mouth to reply with my customary snark when something distracted me just over the shoulder of Cole. Something that made my blood run cold.

"Who is that?" I asked instead.

Everyone turned to looked where I'd indicted then glanced back at me in confusion.

"Who is what? What do you see?" asked Antoine, eyes alert and darting every which way.

"There. Don't you see her? The old woman with milky eyes. And look! Isn't that a pixie flying near her?" I asked in an overexcited but hushed voice. The last thing we needed was people in the area hearing my talk about tiny, menacing imps.

"Nice try, Mags. You can't fool me today!" Dara laughed.

"No really she...whoa! Where did she go?" I gazed around, certain I'd find an old woman hobbling away with pixies zooming hither and yon in her wake. Only no such figure was anywhere in the vicinity and nary a tiny buzzing creature could be found.

"I swear I saw a weird old lady."

"This town is filled with weird old ladies. Shall we?" Cole dismissed my concerns, and it chafed a bit in hindsight—his attitude toward me and my position in the Order was something I hadn't anticipated from Antoine's friend.

We settled up close to the side of the building, the men leaning against the cool interior columns while Dara and I remained under the open arch. I glanced up and read the words music, poetry, art, drama, and athletics that were carved into the stone above my head. I was again saddened that this grand old building remained derelict.

"It's like this. We've had sporadic attacks of zombie-like pixies all throughout the city with Congo Square seeming the epicenter. So far, the residents in the area haven't sighted any nor been affected, but the paranormal community is alarmed."

"I thought the random attacks were more down in the French Quarter?" I asked.

"The last one, yes. Apparently, a shifter I know who works at Café du Monde had two of them dive-bombing him as he left work for the night."

The famous café, open twenty-four hours a day seven days a week, was hardly the place I'd expect marauding pixies to remain unnoticed by a partying populace. But maybe it was due to that very reason the imps remained undetected by the humans too busy getting drunk to notice —even if those humans needed the café to sober up!

"You mentioned zombie-like just now. That's a new occurrence, no?" asked Dara.

"I managed to capture one briefly, and at first it seemed alive and well—or as well as any pixie can be—but when I investigated further, began trying to communicate and had others confront the creature, it began to decay in front of our eyes. Then it zoned out on us and kept attacking, seemingly unaware of what it was doing. You know...zombie-like."

"Where is it now, Cole?" rumbled Antoine, his deep voice barely above a whisper.

"Dead. Literally fell apart on us. Darndest thing I'd ever seen."

"This is good information. We are running blind here not knowing what we are or were up against. The only reason we found out about this pixie problem was thanks to Madame Myna. She'd been conversing with others like her in the many shops in the voodoo district of Bayou St. John, and they informed her of the many attacks."

"I'm sorry...Madame Myna?" asked Cole.

Dara approached the siren and opened her bag slightly, giving Cole a look at the now-glowing crystal ball with Madame swirling around inside.

"Ah. I see. Yes, I can understand now how quickly you grasped our situation. We even had a ruckus over by Marie Laveau's tomb last night."

"She is laid to rest just up the street from here, no?" I asked, remembering that St. Louis #1 was the infamous woman's final resting spot.

"Yes. You can walk to it from here."

"Well, now that we've established we are well aware of your situation in the city, what was it you wanted to speak to us about? This offer," said Antoine.

Cole glanced around looking pensive, but then his face cleared. "Ah, here she comes."

Turning as one, we watched as a willowy Black woman approached all business suit smart and no-nonsense demeanor, but then her face broke out into a broad smile and transformed her into a stunner.

"Cole. Sorry I'm late." The woman gave us a cursory glance and waited for Cole to make the introductions, her focus going back and forth between him and Antoine. OK, then.

"Dalila, this is Antoine, Maggie, and Dara. They are with the antique show here in town."

"Nice to meet you." Another glance our way, but she practically purred when her eyes locked with Antoine's once more. I cocked an eyebrow at him, but he didn't react. Antoine seemed aware of the interest this woman was emitting but remained impassive.

"I'm sure Cole has updated you on this bizarre pixie behavior. I have an offer for your group—just your small circle—not the entire antique section—just the paranormal offshoot."

OK, so this Dalila person was paranormal. I began to scrutinize her in earnest, trying in vain to discern what Breed she might be. I couldn't get a read on her, but Dara looked vexed.

"What is it?" I asked.

Dalila seemed perturbed I spoke up, erroneously assuming Antoine led our small group. I didn't disabuse her of this notion, but let it play out as it would.

"I'd like to make a suggestion. Since Congo Square seems to be a hotbed of pixie activity, and I am on the board on who can and cannot set up shop here and such, I'd like to offer you two days beyond your current schedule to remain in New Orleans and set up your tents here as a cover while you investigate."

That might work out. We didn't have to be to our next location on an urgent time schedule. Our next stop being open to suggestion since we were parting ways for a time with the main troupe. We were hot on the trail of the man we suspected of turning Ellie into a ghost, or revenant rather, and the clues left behind in some items we'd recently come in contact with left us a treasure map of sorts with clues. Clues that led us to New Orleans. Coincidence since we were to arrive in the city as our next stop? The verdict was out on that one for now. But it left a bad taste in my mouth.

"What do you think, Mags?"

Dalila's face registered shock as both her brows raised up into her hairline. She gave me a barely imperceptible once-over, and I almost grinned snidely at her, stopping myself at the last moment.

"We do need time to remain in the city for our *other* situation. Yes, this might work out nicely."

"It would benefit your bottom line as well. Most paranormals hesitate to leave this area, even though Fairgrounds is nearby. You'd probably have quite a turnout of those in the Breed looking to have precious heirlooms appraised, I would think, that aren't from Bayou St. John or close to the racetrack." Dalila flicked her eyes back to Antoine, which made me realize she knew he was from that neighborhood.

"We're here for the week and were supposed to head out on Friday. That would mean us remaining behind to do two days over the weekend here in Congo Square."

"That's right. Saturday and Sunday this place would be yours."

"It's not far from our rental at all," stated Antoine.

"How about we take a vote with the others and see what they say?" suggested Dara.

"No. I think I like this idea. We were planning on remaining behind for a few days anyway...or leaving Antoine and Sven. But now we can all stay and kill two birds with one stone."

"Do you think you can discover the reason behind the pixie problem?" asked Cole.

"We're going to do our best. Something about this is fishy...the smelly kind. There is too much coincidence that we'd be here in New Orleans, have a private matter that would keep a few of us here longer than the rest of the company, and now have marauding pixies added to the mix to keep us distracted," I replied.

"Do you think that's what this is? A distraction?" asked Dara with concern.

"I'm not sure, Dara...but I certainly intend to find out."

Did I mention I don't believe in coincidence?

"Let's head back and talk to our crew," said Antoine.

We said our farewells and promised to update Cole later on that evening with our decision. As we made our way out of Congo Square and back to our waiting vehicle, I couldn't help but glance back to where I'd thought I'd seen the old woman. The place was empty.

But the memory had me peering around, disquieted at the memory.

I know what I saw. I'm sure of it.

Or was I?

CHAPTER 4

*D*inner that evening was lively. We'd all traipsed down to the French Quarter heading to Tujague's, New Orleans oldest restaurant, having been founded in 1856. The Creole fixed price meal was to die for, and I was currently making my way methodically through my veal on pappardelle pasta.

Nathara was sitting across from me frowning.

"I don't like this."

"Don't like what?" I answered, sounding muffled, my mouth full of delicious mushrooms, crawfish, and veal.

"This woman coming out of the blue and offering us a spot on Congo Square. What if she's mixed up in voodoo? Or worse, has an ulterior motive for having us all gathered in one place where we are vulnerable?"

Tor, a fork heaped with mashed sweet potato halfway to his mouth, paused, considering Nathara's words. "When are we ever vulnerable? I think we can handle anything thrown at us...especially in light of who—and what—we are."

"Yes, well...we don't know all that much about this Cole

character nor his friend Dalila. What if it's a trap? We don't know anything about her!"

"She's a lamia."

Antoine's proclamation quieted our table as all eyes turned to him.

"Really? She didn't...I mean, how can you tell?"

"I react oddly to snakes. And that woman exudes snake," he replied.

"And you'd still have us go there? What if Nathara is right, and we've just opened ourselves up to a heap of trouble?" Dara inquired and began biting her lower lip with worry.

"I can handle a lamia," sniffed Bella.

I smacked Tor's hand as he reached over to snag a mushroom out of my plate. "You gnawed your way through two pork chops and all those vegetables. Keep your hands off my meal, mister!"

"I don't believe she is a danger. Cole is a good man, and I trust him," said Antoine.

"Cole, maybe. But Dalila? What if she's bamboozling the guy?" I asked, spearing Tor's brussels sprout and shoving it in my mouth with a look of mischievous triumph.

"I don't think that's the case, but we will keep an eye on her."

"Clue me in here, please," said Ellie, hesitantly. Ever since we'd met up with another vampire, Caliente Saunders, who'd fixed it so that everyone present could see and hear Ellie, she'd reveled in the fact she could partake in our conversations—although watching us eating and drinking had to be tortuous.

"What exactly is a lamia? Is she a snake woman like that Nagini chick in the Harry Potter movies?"

"Fantastic Beasts," said Johnny, our werewolf extraordinaire.

"Fantastic what? Oh, right. So, is she something along those lines?" asked Ellie.

Serena and Sydney raised their hands in tandem.

"Demon," Sydney spoke first.

"Lesser demon. One that devours kids and creepy morphs into a giant, bloated snake," finished Serena.

"I thought they were sea monsters?" asked Sven. Sven was a shifter, and I didn't think he appreciated the derogatory morphing comment.

"All lamia descend from a lessor demon and were sea creatures before the passage of time had them more or less appear human. Lore has the parent as Poseidon, but we know lessor demons created the Breed. Males take on the form of sharks, and females a sea serpent. So basically, they are shifters of a sort," I stated succinctly.

"Someone's been hitting the books! I knew you had to be doing something more than snogging your boyfriend whilst perusing his vast collection of old tomes." Sven winked at me to show he was good-naturedly teasing, although I still blushed scarlet. Sven shifted into a snow leopard and Nathara, while concealing her crossbreed status from many in our group, was not only a dark witch, but part shifter and she transformed into a kestrel. That she was now dating Sven and they had opposing animals was not lost on me. I snickered a bit, thinking of their transformation and subsequent odd pairing...but one that seemed to be working out.

A cat and a bird. Lovely.

"They might have the ability to shift, but they aren't true shifters in the sense of the word. Not like me. Not...ahem, as I was saying..." Sven said, catching himself before he revealed Nathara's secret. "The lamia are oddities in the Breed world because they were created. They did not exist as a Breed before a certain point in time. Their lore is muddied and lost to us, so they remain a mystery."

"Can they be trusted?" Dara, ever the worrywart, looked apoplectic at the thought of doing so.

"I guess we'll find out," drawled Nathara. "But right now, I want to know what we have planned for the rest of the evening? We are off tomorrow, and I want to have some fun."

Yep. Sven is good for our dark witch. Nathara would have been a sullen pain to deal with, but here she was looking to have a grand time in The Big Easy.

"How about we hit that cigar bar around the corner? They advertise they have a huge selection of bourbon. I can't think of anything better than a cigar and a good drink to enhance the taste," said Johnny.

"Listen, lassie. Some of us don't like puffing on a big, black stick. How about we go somewhere else?" Nathara shot back. Yep. There's the dark witch we all love to hate.

"I'd rather we stayed together. Let's hit there first, then we can move on to another place."

"I want to see naked people!" cried Bella.

"And get plastered on Hurricanes," added Sydney. The twins were notorious boozers...but hey, it didn't affect their performance, and I'd never once seen them hungover.

"That means a visit to a burlesque show and drinking Hurricanes at Lafitte's Blacksmith Shop!" cried Bella.

"You're going to get carded," Ellie giggled.

"And isn't that just so ironic?" Bella chortled.

As mentioned, Bella looked forever the bronzed, beach babe teen, bubble gum-popping, and attitude dialed to full snark. But she was probably older than Antoine's mother by a good thousand years, give or take.

"Well, while you guys are getting stupid, I'm going to sniff around the city with the copy of the map. I've been studying it and I think I have some things figured out...but I need to match them up with landmarks," I said.

"We can all do that. The night is young! Let's pay up

here...head to the cigar joint, then onward to a naughty show. By the time we are ten sheets to the wind, drowning in Hurricanes, we'd have probably passed several of your landmarks, Mags. Live a little!"

"Plus, Mom and Dad are here to keep us all in line," snickered Ellie, glancing at Dara and Antoine.

"I'll have you know, I was once asked to perform in a burlesque show!" Dara chided, wagging her finger at Ellie.

"You? Oh, then let's find a place that has open call. Daracha and her sexy moves tonight folks! This I've got to see!" shouted Bella.

And we were off.

* * *

"I'm in love."

Johnny was drooling profusely at the young lady currently stripping, whilst doing her contortionist moves. It was a hybrid strip tease/magic act of sorts and every time the girl bent over, it looked as if a dove flew out of her *ahem!*

Even I could tell she was not only paranormal, but a werewolf to boot, and Johnny had it bad. He reminded me of the wolf howling in delight in those old Looney Tune cartoons while watching a similar show. If he banged on the table and whistled one more time, I would box his ears. Actually, I take that back. There wasn't a cartoon alive that ever depicted a show like this one.

The lovely lady came wriggling over to our table and draped herself artfully across Johnny's lap, whispering something into his ear, and I swear his tongue grew seven inches!

"Down boy. You'll just get fur all over her."

"Steady," Antoine smiled and nodded to the young lady who winked and sauntered off to another table.

"Ugh, why can't I have a nibble?" whined Johnny.

"You know the rules. Look, but no touch!" said Dara.

Tor and Sven had matching bemused smiles on their faces as a redheaded woman dressed in the typical French maid costume paraded around on the left side of the stage. Instead of a feather duster, she had a powder puff in one hand as she fronted a mirror. But instead of staring at herself, she'd locked eyes with my boyfriend and began to slowly strip out of her clothing. Tor's jaw unhinged, and I had the urge to use a napkin to mop up the drool.

"Please. I have a better body than that witch." Nathara was scowling, but not overly upset. She did have a fantastic body and had she decided to hop on stage and remove her clothing, it wouldn't even be a contest. She'd win hands down. Thankfully, she chose to remain seated beside Sven.

"Is it because she's a redhead?" asked Ellie, appearing in front of Tor to partially block his view.

"What? Huh? Oh!" Looking around sheepishly at those of us at the table, he couldn't help but take a sneak peek back at the redhead, then trail his eyes over to my flaming red hair. I smirked and wagged my finger at him. Not today, big boy.

"Probably that and the fact she's a witch like Maggie!" said Bella, who had in fact been carded not once, not twice, but six times already. We had a near riot when a table of college boys from Tulane, every single one of them a sorcerer, lifted Bella up and deposited her on their table for what they called, "a barely legal private show."

Thankfully, the bouncer settled the boys down, but not before Bella flashed them her assets.

Cheeky, that one.

Obviously, we'd wandered into a burlesque that catered to the Breed. Clearly, everyone present was a paranormal being as were the entertainers. It was a fun place where we knew we could relax without the worry of scarring a human with our arcane talents. I briefly wondered how the management kept them out. More than like a charm spell to make them not see the entry or a subtle hint to keep on walking by and hit another establishment instead. Even the college boys have the look of "wizards gone wild" about them.

Unexpectedly, the lights in the place dimmed, and a throbbing music began that hinted of ancient tribal mystery and sounds. Imagine our surprise when Dalila appeared on the stage holding a giant python snake. She was completely naked except for a sparkling charm that dangled round her neck. It looked to be a charm of a small animal, but she was too far away for me to tell what it was—nor did I care. It was, *ahem*, dangling dangerously close to her perky breasts.

Not going there!

OK, then. Suddenly this night became infinitely more interesting.

CHAPTER 5

"*S*he could have told us she was an entertainer!" I grumbled, stomping along Bourbon Street and weaving my way past the drunken revelry. Seriously, didn't this town ever get a break from inebriated tourists meandering along the famous street, upchucking at will and making spectacles of themselves? I guess New Orleans wouldn't be New Orleans without them.

"Why do you care? I mean, when you meet someone new, do you tell them what you do immediately?" asked Bella. "Dalila had no idea we'd show up at her club, anyway. It was just a coincidence we picked the one she works at."

This was true, but again with the coincidence.

"Well, you should have seen her this morning. All business suit and professional looking."

"Maggie Fortune! Don't tell me you've turned into a judgmental prude!" cried Dara.

"I'm not! Not really. I guess. I mean.... grr. Just forget it."

"Ease up on Maggie," Tor spoke up. "I have a funny feeling about tonight myself. The minute Dalila came onto the stage and zeroed in on Antoine, I became suspicious" My hero. "I don't like coincidences, and something didn't sit right with me and the way she acted tonight. Like she knew Antoine would be there and went at him like she was on a mission of some kind."

Antoine, for his part, didn't say a word but continued down the street.

"It seems like Dalila was taunting us with that snake. I'm sure I wasn't the only one who wondered if she'd turn into a snake herself. It was a disturbing performance," I continued.

"It did seem a bit creepy," said Nathara. "She was staring at Antoine like a hypnotist, and I thought she seemed a tad upset he didn't become enamored of her charms."

Everyone else in the club appeared under a trance as she gyrated around the stage going from fully clothed to mostly undressed with the snake strategically placed to keep her from becoming totally nude on stage. Between the lights, music, and illusions flying about, I was surprised the entire audience didn't become permanently under her thrall.

When Dalila realized none in our group held her in the same fashion as the main audience, her focus shifted to the table of college boys, and the moment passed. She didn't come out from backstage to acknowledge our presence after her performance, and that too, was a bit odd.

"I think we lost Sydney." Ellie was floating in front of us like a scout, peering this way and that in search of our missing succubi. Serena was staggering behind us, one shoe off and holding the largest drink I'd ever seen.

"Laugh tits!" Serena snickered, then burped.

"Laugh *what?* Serena, are you OK?"

Throwing her head back and howling at the sky, Serena laughed herself out, then snorted. "Laugh tits! Sydney! Still there."

Turning around and pointing the way we'd come, Serena

managed to convey her message to those of us sober enough to comprehend what she meant.

"Laffite's! Sydney is still at Laffite's Blacksmith Shop?"

When she nodded yes, Johnny broke away from our group and loped off in that direction.

"I'm on it," he said.

Laffite's was one of New Orleans oldest bars, having poured drinks for the populace at large since the 1700s. It was a tiny place, and we'd put a dent in their supply of Hurricanes as well as the strawberry daiquiris. How we managed to overlook Sydney was a mystery. The bar had an intimate setting, with ancient, blackened bricks, old wood beams and a stone floor competing with the skeletons and webs hanging from the ceiling—all fake, thankfully. The skeletons at least, perhaps a few of the spiderwebs were authentic. We'd sat outside in their courtyard at one of the picnic tables...I hope Sydney was still there and had just slipped under one of them or was in the bathroom when we left.

"So, are we going on this treasure hunt then?" asked Sven. He and Nathara had been making googly-eyes at each other and I suspected they'd rather be canoodling back at the hotel then here with me and my makeshift map.

"Not everyone has to come. I can do this myself," I assured them.

Nathara didn't even say a word. She just grabbed Sven's hand and rushed off toward Esplanade Avenue and our building. Dara was blinking slowly, and even Madame Myna's glow was subdued, so I knew they were exhausted.

"Why don't you gather up Serena, Dara, and you can call it a night? Look! Here comes Johnny with Sydney in tow. You can head back to our rental and turn in for the night."

"Found her curled up in the two-way fireplace! Thankfully, it's spring and there's no use for a fire," laughed Johnny, albeit with a bit of a slur and eyes as equally droopy as

Dara's. Sydney was swaying back and forth and had a bemused smile on her soot-covered face.

"Johnny, make sure Sydney gets back to our rental. Dara, you do the same with Serena, then turn in. I'll stay with Maggie," said Antoine, turning an inquiring eye on the rest of our group.

"I'll stay," said Tor.

"Me too!" Bella seemed wide awake, and I wondered if she ever ran out of energy.

Ellie didn't sleep, so she was remaining behind as well, in spectral form of course!

"Can you feed Bob for me, Dara?" The druid nodded yes and waved as she kept her other hand firmly on Serena's elbow, guiding her in the opposite direction from us. My rotund feline would be starving about now—for food and attention—and I knew Dara would give him a little of both.

"Let's head down to Café du Monde, get some coffee, and figure out where this map is leading us," said Tor, putting his arm around my shoulder.

Turning down St. Ann, we walked past the Boutique du Vampyre, and I tilted my head in their direction. "We need to shop there. See if it lives up to Antoine and Tor's expectations, no ladies?"

Bella and Ellie squealed in delight as the men rolled their eyes at us.

"Look! There's even a café!" cried Bella. "I think I know where we're going on our next night off."

Continuing past Place d'Armes Hotel and Muriel's, a classic Creole restaurant popular for their Sunday brunch—and another spot we'd planned on hitting while in town, we reached the famous Jackson Square, which was bustling with people. The church, St. Louis Cathedral, was aglow, and the café ahead lit up with its green-and-white-striped canopy a welcome fixture which gave me a warm feeling. I loved this city so much.

So much so, I wondered why I hadn't suggested our faction didn't relocate down here away from my father's compound in North Carolina, leaving the main antique troupe behind. My father was a thorn in mine and Ellie's side, despite our growing a bit closer in recent months. The dizzying parade of women in and out of his life since our mother's passing did nothing to keep us a close-knit family. If it wasn't for our Aunt Morwena and the various cousins sprinkled around the area, Ellie and I might have run off a long time ago.

Reaching the café, Tor and Antoine wordlessly hit the counter, leaving Bella and me to find a table. Ellie swirled off, and I suspected she'd do some window shopping before joining us once we were settled. Again, watching us partake of hot beignets, liberally sprinkled with powdered sugar, and chicory-laced coffee had to be a trial, and I didn't blame her for not sticking around.

"What did you figure out?" Tor came back to the table with Antoine who held a tray covered in our goodies. Setting a mug of coffee in front of me, he placed one in the spot I'd saved for him and took a seat.

"I know we all worked on deciphering this map on our way down and have many theories, but I think I've figured out the first part at least. It seems to be the easiest, and between Bella, Ellie, and me, I think we know where the first item is."

"Item?" asked Antoine.

"Yes. See here at the end of each passage? There seems to be a tiny drawing, and Ellie thinks it might be a clue to what we need to look for or what type of item we'll find."

"I think it's the image of something we will discover at each location," said Bella.

I glanced around to make sure no one was listening in on our conversation. Other than a waiter close by, no one seemed to be listening in. The place was always crowded and loud, so we could have this talk where it would not have worked in another establishment without someone becoming interesting in what we were saying.

"We need to know where each of these places are around the city." Tor pulled the map toward him, spinning it around so it was right side up. "The first passage says, 'those who live at the RIVER can WALK home to Mama's. She's good for a meal since thirty-eight, and up on the balcony things could be great! The odd one out's loose brick has something inside for you and might contain an additional clue!'

"Those who live at the river. What does that mean?" asked Bella, taking a huge bite out of her beignets, then coughing when the powdered sugar made her choke. A common occurrence in the café apparently, since I'd heard quite a few patrons doing the same thing for the last ten minutes.

"I'm not sure, but river and walk are all in capitals, and that's an obvious nod to *the* Riverwalk here. Mama's is another clue. What's that about?" I wondered aloud, patting Bella on the back.

Antoine whipped out his phone and began tapping away.

"Maybe the clue is on the Riverwalk somewhere," said Tor.

"But then why does it say walk to Mama? Surely Mama must be a place?"

"It is."

We all looked up at the man who'd approached our table —the waiter I'd noticed nearby. He was lanky with a lopsided grin and curly blonde hair that made him look angelic. He had on a white jacket, black bow tie, and a white paper hat with the name of the restaurant on it like the rest of the well-dressed waitstaff were wearing. His moves were graceful, and his eyes darted every which way and twinkled with good-natured cheer.

"I'm Walt. A friend of Cole. He told me you might be in soon."

"How did you know it was us?" I asked.

Walt leaned in close and whispered, "I can tell a vampire a mile away," as he nodded toward Antoine. "Plus, a Black man with ice-blue eyes is kind of easy to spot." He held his hand out and we all shook, my fingers tingling when they connected with his.

"Shifter? Are you something else? I felt..."

"Grab your coffee and beignets and follow me. I know a place we can talk that's more private."

Walt led us out the back of the café to the alley that paralleled Decatur Street, and we walked a few steps until we passed the kitchen coming to another set of doors. These were blacked out so we couldn't see inside.

"Employee break room," explained Walt.

Once we entered, Walt set us up at a break table, and we continued our conversation.

"Care to explain why you were listening in to what we were discussing?" Tor, ever the guardian, queried the young man, who didn't seem all that bothered by the question.

"I had to get close enough to check out Antoine's eyes. Once I verified it was him, I was close...too close, you'd say, and caught the tail end of your discussion. I didn't mean to eavesdrop."

Walt glanced back at me and smiled. "And to answer your question, yes. I'm a shifter, but I have a bit of air elemental in me."

"Air elemental?" Bella cried, "But that means you are part angel?"

"Yep."

That certainly explained the golden curls and stunningly

flawless skin. In my re-education in all things Breed, I'd stumbled upon angel lore and approached Antoine with questions. I assumed angels were myth, but he'd informed me he had a cousin by marriage that was one as well. Or part anyway. He'd described her as having stunning curls, impeccable skin as dark and smooth as melted chocolate, and rich copper-brown eyes flecked with gold that seemed to look into your soul.

Angels just look like angels! This guy was no exception, and that little zing I felt when our hands met was my psychic ability letting me know I'd found one—even through my leather gloves.

"Walt, you said something about their being a place that relates to our puzzle here. The word 'mama?' What do you know?"

"Actually, I know two things. You mentioned, 'those who live at the river.' I know exactly what that is describing, but it's not because I'm some kind of puzzle genius or anything," he said with a self-deprecating smile.

"I think you're being modest, but go on," I said.

"It's the meaning behind one of our street names—a famous, and highly unpronounceable one to most tourists. Tchoupitoulas Street. In Choctaw, it means exactly that—those who live at the river."

"Wow! Really?" squealed Bella. "That's so neat. It's one puzzle answered."

"No... two," continued Walt. "The 'Mama' reference must mean Mother's!" He sat back proudly like he'd answered the world's greatest riddle, but I looked at him in confusion.

"Mother's?"

"It's a storied restaurant near Canal Street. I know it well," said Antoine, beaming. "Of course. You can "walk" to Mother's from the new Riverwalk shops. And Mother's has a balcony. I believe it is on Poydras Street."

"You are correct!" Walt exclaimed.

"Now might be a good time to head over since the cover of night might allow us a chance to continue the search unhindered, but as it's on a busy corner, we may have to tread carefully. Before we go, what can you tell us of the pixie attack that happened here?" Antoine gave Walt his full attention, and it gave me time to study the young man.

He definitely looked like an angel, but I couldn't figure out what kind of animal he shifted into. Some are easy. Our Johnny was a wolf shifter and one look at him would convince you of that. He's one tall, dark, and handsome dude with a mane of black hair, and the nicest and whitest teeth I've ever seen on a man. GQ would drool to have him on their cover. Johnny creamed wolf.

Sven was a snow leopard, and his Nordic mien was aloof, predatory, and catlike. He was a silent enigma. If I had to cast someone to play a cat burglar, Sven would be my first choice.

Nathara was a shock to me when it was revealed she also had shifter in her. Now that I know, I could see how a kestrel was her spirit animal. Beautiful, swift, and deadly described her perfectly.

Walt? Not so much. Maybe it was because his angelic façade concealed his inner beast—it certainly kept me wondering. He was graceful but not in any way catlike. He had presence and a regal bearing but not over the top, with large, slow-blinking eyes that seemed to take everything in. He was certainly breathtaking but had a wall up, despite his friendly demeanor...almost like he commanded respect but would as soon dash off as remain in one place if things got too much for him. He definitely gave off solitary vibes. When Walt spoke to you, he gave his undivided attention and you were drawn to his eyes, and everything and anyone else faded to the background. It was a heady sensation.

Tapping my fingers across my lips, I kept scrutinizing the man as he replied to Antoine's query.

"It was the weirdest thing. I was just leaving my shift and heading home for the evening when right out of nowhere this pixie came at me, tearing at my eyes, all teeth and ferocity. I mean, come on! A pixie? I managed to smack it away, which gave me plenty of guilt, mind you. They are such small creatures, but had I not, I'm not sure my eyes would have survived!"

"Did it go away after you hit it?" asked Bella.

"That's another thing odd. No. It chased me to that fountain on the other side of this pathway." Walt nodded his head toward the Instrument Men fountain at the far end of the alley that separated the two long buildings which housed the tourist shops, Café du Monde anchoring the other end.

"I got to the fountain and the little pixie hit the ground and began a jagged walk toward me acting a bit zombie-like before collapsing on its side. Then two other pixies came out of nowhere to rush to their fallen comrade's aid. They lifted him up and flew off to heaven knows where. That's the last I saw of them."

"Can you show us the spot?" asked Tor, who seemed on edge.

"Sure, it's just outside to our left." Walt led the way, taking us back outside and we wandered to the open area where the fountain sat, a few tourists sitting nearby talking or drinking coffee while watching the water display.

"It's a much-maligned fountain, really," Walt offered. "Usually, it's covered in bird poop and faded, but every once in a while, the city officials send someone out here to paint it and it comes to life."

Tor began wandering the area, looking up, down and every which way. I wasn't sure if he assumed a pixie would show up and begin terrorizing us, but he had a pensive look, remaining alert and very much on guard.

Walt was showing Bella a map of Mother's on his phone, leaving me alone with Antoine, who rubbed his chin, deep in thought.

"What is it?" I asked.

"This is a busy area, even back here behind the shops. I'm surprised no tourists or locals reported seeing something unusual, and it's not being talked about. Does it mean only paranormals can see them?"

"Can humans see pixies?"

"I don't know why not. I mean...usually they keep themselves out of sight, but there is nothing concealing them should they choose to show themselves. Thankfully, they are usually frightened of humans and stay away from them."

"Which means something—or someone—is sending them out and about to run amok."

"There's another thing to consider," said Antoine. "Whoever is doing this—controlling the pixies—there is also the possibility they are cloaking them so only we, and by we, I mean Breed, only we can see them."

"That's a lot of magical energy to expend," I huffed out in a massive sigh.

"Which means whoever is behind this is extremely powerful."

Great. Just what we need...not.

CHAPTER 6

$\mathcal{N}$othing much happened while Tor was scouring the area looking for *something*, and Walt was getting restless.

"I need to get back to work, or my manager will give me heat."

Just as we were about to say our farewells, Nathara rounded the corner and stopped short.

"What are you doing here?" she asked.

"I can say the same to you."

"I asked first."

We took the time to introduce her to Walt, who appeared instantly smitten. Nathara has that happen more often than not. Certainly, everyone could tell he would rather have stayed behind and chatted her up even as he reluctantly strolled back to the café, giving us one final wave.

"You sure made an impression," I said to Nathara who'd tracked Walt's progression away from us.

"Don't I always?"

I guess. Grr.

"He seems nice."

"Yeah...for a shifter."

"I wonder what kind he is?" I asked, not expecting a reply from the dark witch.

"Easy. He's an owl."

"An owl? How can you tell?"

Nathara gave me a pitying look and shook her head.

"Trust me. I can tell."

I decided to change the subject, bringing the conversation back to why she was here in Jackson Square and not cuddling with Sven back at the rental.

"He passed out from exhaustion and too many daiquiris," she sighed. "So I thought I'd do a little sightseeing—then I smelled the beignets."

Ah, yes. The beignets.

"Well, we have a lead on the first clue on that map. We thought since the night is young, for us anyway, we might as well see where it takes us. Apparently, it's down near Canal Street and the shops at Riverwalk."

"What are we waiting for then? Let's go!"

We decided to hoof it since Antoine stated Mother's Restaurant was only about seven or so city blocks from the square. He'd never been but was familiar with the name and the area. We updated Nathara on what Walt had told us, and she was curious to see what we'd find at the location but didn't think the pixie attack warranted our concern yet. "A few pixies attacking one of us doesn't stand a chance."

But what if they came in the hundreds? Thousands? And was it fair to the pixies if someone was compelling them to misbehave like this? And to what end?

Once we'd arrived outside the restaurant, now closed due to the late hour, we began to examine the exterior, which did indeed have a tiny wrought iron balcony on the second floor. There was no way the old structure would support all of us upon it, so we decided to let Bella head up once we figured out a way to get her there—she was tiny and the only one wearing all black, good to remain undetected in the shadows.

We continued to the corner of Tchoupitoulas, then turned on Poydras and walked the length of the building to the parking lot. There we discovered the building has a kind of stepped structure which would allow Tor or Antoine to boost Bella up, then follow, getting her to the upper level where she could then drop down onto the balcony.

"I'm looking for something that is 'the odd one out,' and something is under a loose brick, right?" asked Bella.

"The entire building is made out of bricks. Good luck with that!" snickered Nathara unhelpfully.

"Actually, I think it's going to be rather easy," sniffed Ellie, giving support and causing Nathara to scowl in her direction.

"Why do you say that El?" I asked.

"Look up there on this side of the building!"

We looked to where Ellie was pointing and noticed four diamond-shaped protrusions embedded into the brick. I believed them to be earthquake restraints, or some kind of iron or steel additions to keep the building from shifting. Antoine agreed with my assessment. Three of them were in a perfect row in a diamond shape—point up and point down—as mentioned, but the last one was definitely the odd one out —it was rotated to look like a square. The four equal-length sides were definitely turned so it was flat on top and bottom. An error during construction or a deliberate act, we'd never know...but hopefully Bella would find a loose brick directly under it.

This should be a piece of cake!

Trying to remain unobtrusive as we casually sauntered to the back of the parking area, we nonetheless waited another ten minutes to make sure no one had noticed us loitering around and called the police. We needn't have worried. All was quiet and the coast, as it were, remained clear. When we finally felt certain we could attempt the climb without getting caught, Antoine signaled for Bella to move forward.

"Wait. How will we do each level? This first one is easy...Tor is here to boost Antoine up. But what about the next level?" Bella stood there looking toward the roof and scratching her head.

"Oh, for the love of..." Nathara rolled her eyes and pointed to Tor. "OK, big guy. Lift Bella onto your shoulders so she can get on this first platform, and I can do the rest."

Tor and Antoine shared the duty of hoisting Bella up so she could scramble over the edge and onto the roof. Then before we could turn to see what Nathara had planned, we saw a trickle of magic shoot past us and circle Bella. The magic made it easy to float Bella up the additional levels then gently set her down. Now all she had to do was drop down onto the balcony and find the loose brick.

"We didn't think to use magic. I mean if someone saw us..."

"Then they'd have something to tell their shrink. The longer we stand out here looking suspicious, the better the chance we get caught!" huffed Nathara.

She had a point.

Bella quickly dropped out of sight, and we assumed she'd made it to the balcony. We didn't hear any screams from the street or hear traffic screeching. We dared not head around the building to watch her progress, certain a small group of people staring up at a closed restaurant would garner the attention we were trying to avoid.

"I hope she found something," I said.

"She will." Antoine seemed rather confident on the matter.

"Let's just hope she thinks to use magic to wriggle that

brick out or we'll be here all night," grumped Nathara. "I mean she..."

"YEAOW! Get away from me!"

Bella shrieking into the night caused all of us to jump and tear around to the front of the building. Witnesses be damned...our friend might be in trouble!

"Whoa! Where did she go? Where's Bella?" I asked.

"Right there. How can you miss...wait? That's not Bella. What the heck is that?" asked Nathara, unable to hide the horror from creeping into her voice.

What now stood on the balcony where we knew Bella had been was a rail thin man, short in stature, but thin to the point of emaciation. He was lumbering around, making jerky movements, and moaning slightly.

"He looks like, but no...it can't be."

"He looks like a zombie," I cried. "Just say it Nathara. That's a slipping zombie!"

"Calm down, Mags. We don't know what that is yet," said Tor gently.

"Calm down! Calm down? How can I calm down? Bella should be standing there holding a brick in her hand. You heard her! Now all we have is a creeping, undead loser moaning in her place, and you want me to calm down?"

"Where is Bella? This isn't good," said Antoine.

Oh, you think? I mean, how much worse can it get?

Just then, a patrol car pulled over to the curb and the window retracted, allowing one of the officers inside to peer out and question us.

OK...it can get worse.

"Howdy, officer. How can we help you?"

"We got a report in about a disturbance near Mother's and I just found y'all out here standing around. Care to tell me what you're doing?"

I fought the urge to glance over to the balcony where the

zombie—I refused to think it could be anything else—was still ambling back and forth, moaning with arrhythmic movements like a puppet on strings. Why hadn't the officers noticed it?

"Oh, you know us tourists. We forget that the rest of the populace at large needs their beauty sleep," said Nathara, turning the charms up a notch. I watched as both officers went slack-jawed as they turned to see who was speaking. Nathara has her uses.

It still didn't explain their lack of noticing the flipping zombie just over their shoulder, especially when the darned thing managed to topple over the wrought iron railing and face-plant onto the sidewalk below.

CHAPTER 7

"*L*ook, lady. I don't have all day. Is this worth anything or not?"

The man standing in front of me tapping his foot with impatience at my lack of speed, held up the tattered copy of The Fountainhead and flapped it back and forth in front of my nose. Had the book been worth anything—it wasn't—and were it something to keep in pristine condition —again, it was too far gone to ever be considered good, let alone pristine—I would have already had it safely in my possession. But if the book was worth a dollar in its current condition, and the fact that it was a common paperback copy? Yeah. No value there.

I felt a migraine settling in behind my eyes and frowned at the clueless wonder in front of me. After last night, I didn't have much sympathy for irate customers nor felt any semblance of the warm and fuzzies toward Estelle who'd called us into work despite it being our day off. Apparently, quite a few paranormals showed up with precious family heirlooms to be evaluated.

Jethro Stubbins was not among them.

"Now don't you go givin' me that look, sha. You just bein' prejudiced on account of me bein' Cajun, and dat just wrong."

"I can guarantee I am not being the slightest bit prejudiced on account of your Cajun ancestry."

"But my parrain gave me this copy and told me it held a lot of value!" argued Jethro, his manner getting more and more agitated, causing Bella to go wide-eyed as he began hopping up and down.

"Parrain?"

"You know parrain! Godfather!"

"Well, I'm sorry to tell you this, but your parrain was wrong. This book is only worth a few dollars at best. Perhaps he meant the knowledge you'd gather from reading the book." Yeah, right, because The Fountainhead was such an esteemed tome—not.

"Read it? He wouldn't do dat to me! He knows I can't read none!"

"I'm sorry to hear that. I really am. Maybe you should keep it and ask him to read it to you," I suggested gently.

"C'est fou! The man's been dead goin' on twenty years now!"

"Well, then, you can't rightly ask him to read it now, can you?" said Bella. "Unless of course you want to see if one of our mediums—we have one or two who think they have a touch of the gift—can call him from the other side and see if he'd like his book back."

"Don't be talkin' foolish, cher! Now you've gone and given me the frissons! I don't want no spirit botherin' me. I'll just take this to someone else, don't know why I bothered askin' no woman!"

"I'm sorry I was of no use to you," I said.

"Don't be condescending me now, cher. I might be Cajun, but I know what some of you are. You think I can't see that child over there? She a revenant? And that young man in the furniture tent. I know he be a rougarou. And you. You think I can't tell a sorcière when I see one? We have lots of strange folks in this city. I'm sure you've seen your fair share already!"

What? He can see Ellie? And sorcière sounded enough like a sorceress for me to comprehend he meant witch. Rougarou had me thrown but Jethro knows that we are paranormal, and it sent shockwaves through me, Bella, and Ellie.

"I'm not sure I know what you mean," I stated weakly.

"You just keep your eyes peeled then, sha. I'm certain you'll run in to all manner of odd folk. We sure do have a surplus of the outré in New Orleans. Turn the corner and see a ghost, turn another and there be a creepy old lady givin' you the evil eye. It's part of the charm! Au revoir!"

We watched as Jethro headed out after giving us a knowing smile and proceeded to meander around the booths until he found one of our old book dealers—not Tor, who I should have called, and our expert in all things old books— but a human who had quite a vast collection of hardcovers and paperbacks in his possession and would hopefully deflate Jethro's hopes that his book was of any worth.

"It's New Orleans. I'm telling you! I do keep running into people giving me the evil eye, or the stink-eye...or just plain odd looks! So much so, I've taken to wearing a mirrored reflector, so any hexes are sent back at them!" cried Bella. "Like those cops last night. I still don't know how they missed a zombie falling out of the sky and practically landing on top of them. Yet when I walked around the side of the building after escaping that lunatic who tried to throw holy water on me in that top floor apartment I stumbled into, what do they do? Cross themselves and beg me to 'pardon' them, then take off!"

Not only had Bella shown up looking a little bedraggled and worse for wear due to fighting off a crazed tenant—she'd tumbled into the window after the zombie dude appeared, but the window she jumped through happened to be the home of a religious zealot who had crosses carved into his arms and rosary beads of all shapes and sizes on every single surface. When Bella came crashing in, he assumed the worst, calling her a demon—he wasn't that far off her being an earth elemental—and started dousing her in holy water.

It took us a few minutes to wipe his brain of the memory of Bella, then hunt down the zombie who'd jerky-walked his way to the Mississippi River and was stuck trying to figure out how to climb the steps to the water's edge. When we ascertained he was in fact undead, we let Bella dispatch him to the other side, but not before he managed to come apart in the most explosive way imaginable. We think he might have sneezed!

Yeah...go figure.

Parts of him flew off and hit us when he did. It didn't kill him...I mean, he was already undead. So Bella just put him on another plane and hoped he'd run into something worse over there that could nullify his bad mojo—or patch him up.

What else were we supposed to do? Not one of us believed zombies were real. Imagine our shock.

Even Antoine was pale as a ghost when we discovered the truth—and that's saying something, all things considered.

The night wasn't a total failure however. Bella managed to find the loose brick, pull it away from the side of the building and nabbed the item inside—a minuscule gris-gris, a local protection spell in the shape of a leather necklace with a matching pouch that held some charms, a feather, and a talon of some sort, along with a scroll. On the scroll was some kind of spell but we hadn't had a chance to study it yet. All were safely tucked into the wall safe back at our unit.

But the most frightening part of last night? Just before we'd cleared out and returned to our rental, I glanced up at the balcony above Mother's Restaurant and could swear I saw the figure of an old lady. The same one who appeared in Congo Square, if I was not mistaken. Instead of saying anything, I chalked it up to being overtired and let it go. Now I wish I hadn't.

Creepy old ladies indeed!

I had to quickly put on my professional smile as the next person in line came in and this time, I knew without a doubt I was in the presence of another paranormal. First of all, this man practically emitted magical charges and for another, whatever he was carrying in the wooden box he held gave me such a case of the willies I almost pushed back my chair and ran from the tent. I said almost, because I am definitely too curious for my own good and needed to know what he had in his possession.

"Good afternoon. May I inquire as to whom I have the pleasure of attending to my needs today? Miss Maggie or Miss Ellie?"

I kept the smile plastered to my face even as my eyes widened in shock. "I'm sorry...do I know you?"

"Augustus Kingsley, at your service, Miss...?"

"I'm so sorry. Maggie Fortune." I held my gloved hand out and the man shook it, noting the leather that separated us from touching but not commenting on it.

"I am a friend of your Aunt Morwena, but alas, I haven't been in the States for a few decades. I'd heard that her nieces. Maggie and Ellie ran the appraisal business, leaving her retired and William free to pursue his, um...other interests."

Ah, yes, my father and his skirt-chasing ways proceeded him.

"Of course, but you must have heard my sister Ellie passed, I'm sorry to say."

"I was under the impression she was under the weather...that was the last correspondence I had from Morwena. I am sorry to hear this, my dear."

I nodded my thanks then glanced down at his parcel. "May I help you with something?"

As he sat the item down on my table, I wondered what the future would be like should we manage to return Ellie back to her corporeal state and she was no longer a ghost. We were informed that she'd forever be a revenant, but would be a living, breathing witch once more and could call on her new powers to basically cross between the veils and go into ghost form. A neat trick, and one we fervently hoped for soon. But how to tell the world at large—or at least the paranormal one—of her return without it causing too much scrutiny? I certainly hadn't informed The Order of Origin of my intentions nor that I'd sided with an ancient vampire and a ghost-hunter, she herself a revenant, in the search for the identity of the man who'd turned Ellie. Call it a side project if you will. One without the blessing of the Order.

Setting aside my thoughts and focusing on the object on the table, I tuned into Augustus Kingsley and the tale he was telling.

"So you see, I am a bit of a collector of rare and unusual. Now mind you, I rarely deal in the fantastical, but I came across this item last week and knew I needed to have it appraised and assessed for...otherworldly, shall we say, influences."

"Does he suspect whatever it is might be possessed?" whispered Ellie from her perch on a stool across the tent.

Bella, who shared my tent, shrugged and cut her eyes to me. I flicked mine to Ellie, giving her an "I'm not sure," response.

I watched as Augustus opened the box and removed a cloth-covered object. Setting it down on my table, I could hear a soft hum and the soft breath of faraway voices hinting at something malevolent. My heebie-jeebies hadn't eased up. In fact, they accelerated, matching the beating of my heart which I'm sure sounded like a drum at this point.

Folding back a purple velvet cloth, Augustus exposed an old tome. Blacked with age and vibrating with power, I knew I was out of my league and needed the expert in such things —namely Tor—to help me figure out what we had here. But I couldn't resist running my hands across the beautifully detailed cover despite it being carved with all manner of unsettling figures. Slipping off one glove as if in a trance, I resumed petting the tome and felt myself sucked far away into another place and time.

"You don't belong here. But how interesting that you could join me."

I blinked a few times until my eyesight cleared up from the blurry vision, and I locked eyes with a strange woman.

I'd never seen anyone like her before. Not tall but carrying herself in such a way she appeared statuesque despite being shorter than me, her eyes bore into mine with a strange glow I'd not seen in another being. They flashed and went from a periwinkle to violet and were absolutely mesmerizing. Her hair was long... like all the way down to her ankles long, and dark brown with a streak of stark white striped across one side of her head. I briefly thought of Lily Munster, then tossed that away...this woman was even more striking than the television character—not disparaging Yvonne de Carlo, but she couldn't hold a candle to the visage in front of me.

But it was her mouth that had me drawing back in alarm. Sharp razor-like teeth showed when she spoke, and I remained dumbstruck despite her continued queries.

"Do you know where you are and with whom you are speaking?"

I managed to shake my head no, not taking my eyes off those teeth for a second.

"My name is Discordia, and this is my kingdom."

Kingdom? Then I wasn't in some past time looking at a memory attached to that book? I actually transported to another place?

Pulling my eyes from Discordia's face, I glanced around and noted how bizarre the terrain appeared. Some things looked familiar. The rocks and boulders nearby and the pond with water lilies floating on them in which Discordia occupied the centers, perched on a gilded chair upholstered in crushed velvet in a deep shade of purple—not unlike the fabric Augustus had wrapped around the book.

"What kingdom is this?" I asked.

"Ninfea. It is the land of the nyx."

As she spoke, all manner of creatures appeared around her, and I gasped when I realized most of them appeared to be pixies of some sort—a massive number of pixies all with highly irate dispositions. It left no doubt of my welcome here —I wasn't. These were nothing like Chuck's friends. While the pixies, albeit choleric and misshapen unlike the ones of which I was familiar, these other creatures were so fantastical I don't think any books in my collection would do them justice.

"I don't understand."

"How could you? A mere witch. I come to you now, in this way, to give you a warning. You've tainted my kingdom and I order you to remove this infection before it does even more damage than it already has done!"

"I've tainted your kingdom? But I've never been here before. Heck, I've never heard of it! How could I have tainted it?" I asked.

Just then a row of smallish horse-like creatures appeared with hideous beings astride them. I felt revulsion of a kind I'd never believed possible—and that was saying something having had just battled the exploding zombie! They made growling, gnashing sounds, and the hair on my arm went on high alert.

Upon closer inspection, I noted their lack of skin...both rider and beast—they were all muscle and sinew, slick and oozing with some unknown substance, and oh how they reeked! Then my stomach lurched, and I came close to losing my lunch when I realized those weren't riders, they were fused into one body like some kind of freakish centaurs, but with both a horse-like head and a humanoid one. Now I had goosebumps—fissures—like Jethro had mentioned, and I wanted to turn tail and get as far away from them as possible.

Instead, I swallowed the bile that arose in my throat and croaked out a question of my own. "What are they?"

"Many of your kind call them nuckelavee. But in my world, they are the direnokk."

"And what is it they do exactly?" I asked, dreading the answer.

"They gather the dead, strip them of flesh and send them on their way to the next life."

I blinked in confusion. "I've not heard of any such creature. I thought angels were in charge of..."

"Let me make myself clear. The direnokk do not bother with those that cross from your world into ours in death. They seek out the abominations who would try and cheat death, take their flesh—they covet the skin, you see—and use their bones for magic, sending the soul off to wherever after a painful and joyous killing. Joyous for the direnokk, they do so love to shred flesh of the living."

"I don't understand. Who do they hunt? What type of being tries to cheat death?"

"Why, revenants of course."

And Ellie just happens to be one. Suddenly I didn't like where this was going, and I knew I was miles out of my league in dealing with this Discordia chick.

Where was my team when I needed them?

CHAPTER 8

"*A*nd she just let you leave?" asked Nathara, her brow cocked in disbelief.

We were back in our rental after most of my team closed up shop and escorted me home. Needless to say, I gave them all a scare—even the dark witch—and Nathara's brusque attitude, while on full display, could not conceal the worry she'd shown when Tor came rushing over to the group tents carrying my seemingly lifeless body. I'd fainted pretty quickly after my return, despite babbling incoherently for a full minute.

"After she showed me Ellie's body all laid out on a platform not unlike the one in Aunt Morwena's basement."

"I don't understand. I thought my body was here, on this plane. How could it be in some fairy realm surrounded by those nasty nunchuks?" Ellie cried.

"Nuckelavee."

"Whatever!"

"And it *is* here. But somehow it is there in Ninfea as well," I said.

"Wow. I've heard of the place but thought it was lore...made-up stuff. You know how things get all mucked up even among the Breed," said Bella.

"But I thought Joan of Wad ruled the pixies, no? Isn't she the pixie queen?" asked Dara.

"In Cornish folklore. But let's face it, there are so many other places with their own fae stories. From what I can tell, Discordia is the queen of the nyx...or dark pixies. Maybe Joan is her sister or something, and sweet, and she rules the nice pixies like Chuck," I stated. It sounded like an interesting fairy tale to me anyway.

"Don't be a dunderhead, Mags. All pixies are a nuisance!" declared Dara with a harrumph.

I scowled at Dara but didn't comment. I was too comfortable what with being draped across Tor, my back against his broad chest as he stroked my hair gently. Hey! I was punted back into this world by those lousy nyx and took quite a tumble out of my chair, startling Bella, and Ellie...not to mention Augustus Kingsley, who appeared apoplectic when I began raving about predatory skinless horses.

He'd gladly sold us the tome for a tidy sum of money and wished us well, sending his best to my Aunt Morwena—then took off at a rapid pace far away from the crazy woman.

Me. I'm the crazy woman.

I never did figure out what Breed he was. But my money was on a lower class of witch. More practicum spells and potions and less natural abilities. And there was any reason to be ashamed of this—he just didn't have much power once separated from that book. It now resided in a locked trunk Antoine kept for just such instances—not that we'd ever come across a book that allowed entry into a fairy realm before!

"I'd like to point out that you mentioned the queen stated

Ellie is corrupt and is neither revenant nor witch, or in this case, let's say human. The nyx are upset because, while her body resides in their realm, they cannot touch her. We assume this is because of the protective measures Aunt Morwena put up to guard Ellie's body lest she is able to come back fully on our side." Tor paused to consider what he'd said, then sighed before continuing.

"Normally, I suspect once a body is interred it loses any chance of becoming a revenant. But those already revenants by birth or made, as in Ellie's case, once passed, go into the nyx realm where they are consumed, bones ground up for magical concoctions, and the soul of the person moves on to another life."

"But that's horrid!" cried Ellie. Even if I'm brought back, I will be a full revenant. That's what Samantha Geist told me. I don't want to grow old and die and be eaten by skinless horses!"

We all commiserated with Ellie but didn't know quite what to say.

"What will happen to Ellie if she's brought back to life? I mean, what will happen to the body in the nyx realm?" asked Nathara.

Sydney and Serena glanced warily at each other but didn't say a word. Even Bella was subdued.

Finally, Bella sighed and scratched the side of her nose in frustration—it was a stalling technique, and I watched as she gathered her thoughts.

"OK, here's the thing. We three," Bella indicated herself as well as Serena and Sydney, "are all from other planes than this one. What we know of fae lore is far more than most, but still meager compared to what the verity of their vast world is like."

Bella stood and began to pace around. "The revenants are

few and far between. Very rare in our world, but they do exist. Most are related in some way. Samantha Geist—her surname means ghost by the way—is from a storied family, well respected and all prolific at what they do."

"Hunt ghosts? Those who escaped crossing over to the next life for one reason or another and are stuck here?" asked Sven.

"Precisely. I know other family names, Sepulchre, Morbus, Grimwalker, Spectra, and many more who are dedicated to the task of finding these souls and moving them on before...um..." Bella looked at the twins.

"Before our kind, well, not succubae like Serena and me, but other demons, those who are tasked with nabbing recalcitrant souls or ones who've made a pact, come to take the poor fools who now have quite a price on their head and drag them into hell."

"But that's horrible! Those poor souls, for one reason or another, became confused, then got too scared to leave what they found comfort in. If Samantha and others like her don't get to them first, they are bound to hell for all eternity? I can't believe you demons!" cried Ellie.

I thought of a few of the ghosts I knew, Lily's friend, Edith, my grandmother, Moira, to name a couple...and wondered what would become of them if Samantha—or worse—one of her demon counterparts nabbed them. It was a sobering thought. And I, as head of our secret division of monster-hunters here in the US, needed to find out.

"Calm down, sweet cheeks," grinned Sydney. "What most people don't realize is that souls don't spend eternity in hell. They go for an extended visit, get in a long line for a new host body and poof! Back to try it all over again."

"Yeah," agreed Serena, "if everyone knew this, we'd have triple the baddies running around knowing their souls are safe."

"I wouldn't say safe," said Bella with an evil glint in her eye I'd never seen before. "Each trip into hell makes it harder to climb that rung and reach salvation. I know souls who have been there going on three thousand years now. And until they achieve some kind of true transformation and can start the reset process, there they will remain. It's why most of the upper demons despise those who make it their life's mission to be soul catchers."

"Like that horrid Pandora," said Sydney with venom.

"Dorie is an amazing person! She's sweet and kind. She..."

"She will barter for your soul...even yours, Ellie...and not bat an eye if you don't watch out. It's in her nature. She can't help what she is—and I, for one, want no part of her," said Serena.

"Can I ask a question?" When no one said anything to the contrary, I took the time to consider my words, then tentatively asked what could possibly become a volatile situation.

"Why do you three detest Pandora, really? Is it because she tricks souls? But no... forgive me for being blunt, but Sydney...Serena...you entice men to do naughty things in their sleep. For every successful encounter, they lose time on the 'good side' and can find themselves in hell...no?"

"Yeah...so?"

"So how is that so different from Pandora?"

The three women in question looked as if they'd been slapped.

"Maggie, you don't understand. Pandora isn't a lessor demon. She's up there with the big guns and has very few she answers to. But even her superiors fear her. She's a loose cannon. Totally unpredictable and untouchable in our plane," said Bella.

"Why is that?" I asked.

"Why...she's who you know of as Lucifer's firstborn child. Serena, Sydney, and I have a code of conduct we must follow," Bella continued. "But Pandora? She writes her own laws. She makes up her own canon. Pandora is truly like her namesake and the bringer of doom upon earth. Pandora is chaos."

I looked at Ellie.

She looked down at her spectral hands.

"You sure can pick some friends."

"Then why is she working as a crossroads demon?" Ellie asked.

"Perhaps she likes to slum around gathering lowlifes who'd sell theirs for a wad of cash, or the girl of their dreams. You know the type," said Johnny.

No. you didn't have to be a lowlife to sell your soul. Just horribly desperate and at the end of your rope.

"I think Pandora likes to find the person so far off the path of righteousness they are about to lose it all...but at the last minute they redeem themselves and back out of the deal," said Ellie. "Go ahead and laugh at me, but I know Dorie better than all of you."

"People, can we get back to the matter at hand? What did this nyx queen want with you, Mags? And how did she know we'd be here? I assume she is behind the pixie menace?" asked Antoine.

"She wants us to remove the taint...namely Ellie, who is an aberration in her world, and allow them to cleanse the area. Apparently, with Ellie there in her vegetative state, the nuckelavee cannot feed and are withering away. The pixies too. Which is why she's sent them to this side of the veil to cause chaos of their own. But here's the thing...Discordia said she became aware of our tie to Ellie because of Chuck. She has no idea why the pixies are out of control in New Orleans but has her suspicions."

"What does she need from us?"

I sighed, already knowing the response I'd get when I'd tell them what was up."

"The queen of the nyx requires the soul of a voodoo queen in trade for Ellie's. Only then will she call back the menacing pixies and they will go back to normal."

CHAPTER 9

"*A*re you kidding me? There is no way we can possibly take out a voodoo queen, if there even is such a thing, and serve her up on a silver platter to appease Discordia. We don't murder for hire!" cried Johnny, incensed that someone would assume we'd kill at will. "We are monster-hunters and we eliminate evil. We don't take on marks like hitmen!"

"Are there any voodoo queens, Antoine? I know Marie Laveau was purported to be one in her day, but today?" asked Sven. He'd been quiet for so long I wondered if he'd dropped off—he had his head back and his eyes closed for much of the conversation.

"There are rumors. I mean, we exist contrary to the popular belief of most humans, so why not a voodoo queen? Just because none of us have run across one before doesn't mean there isn't such a thing," replied Antoine.

"Hang on a minute. If Discordia's not behind the pixies running wild, who is? And if she can call them back, it suggests she still has control over them...or...wait. Is that why she wants a voodoo queen? Is that who is behind the craziness?" asked Nathara.

"That is what Discordia told me. She said a voodoo queen has cast a spell on some of her nyx causing them to misbehave—more than what is normal, anyway. They are already fragile because of Ellie's taint in their realm and are growing weaker and easy to manipulate. Whoever this woman is, she is dabbling in some dark mumbo-jumbo and has now moved on to zombies—as evidenced by our friend last night."

"But where would we even begin finding this woman? New Orleans is filled with those pretending to be some kind of voodoo priestess. But a queen?" Dara looked as flummoxed as I felt. "In two days, we move to Congo Square...the purported hot bed of voodoo practitioners. Is that when this woman will show herself—if ever? I mean, she doesn't even know about us, right?"

I thought of the mysterious old woman with the milky white eyes and shivered.

"About that. Remember the other day when we met with Cole at Congo Square?" This I addressed to Antoine who nodded yes. "And remember when I asked about an old woman? You all laughed it off dismissing what I thought I saw. But that's just it guys, I really did see an old woman with a milky white film over her eyes...and there was a pixie swirling around her head. Then she just up and disappeared. What if she is the woman behind all of this?"

"Perhaps, Maggie. But one sighting of a strange woman..."

"No. She was at Mother's as well. Just as we were leaving after dealing with that zombie thing, as we passed by Mother's on our trek back home, I saw her again. She was up on the balcony this time."

"And you didn't say anything, woman?" Antoine was shocked.

"And have you brush it off again like the last time? I

thought perhaps I was overtired and my brain was playing tricks on me. After all, you, and Dara...even Cole...didn't see her when I pointed her out that day. Maybe I'm the only one who can see her!"

"This isn't good. I don't like this at all," said Tor, pulling me tighter against his chest. "This person is targeting Maggie. We need to do something...I..." Tor growled without finishing his thought.

I could feel his heart thumping against his chest and his concern for me was touching. I could sense his fear, however, and I didn't want him to freak out. His half vampire kept him aloof in most dire situations, but the sorcerer half tended to bring out the worst in Tor when he felt someone he loved was being threatened. Not to mention how possessive vampires are! When all hell broke loose around us, Tor tended to get overprotective, and the last thing I needed was him calling the Order trying to have me pulled from this case and kept in a safehouse somewhere!

Not that he'd ever done that in the past, but now with our new status as a couple, he got weird every time danger was afoot.

I knew he couldn't help it. Men get that "need to protect" thing going, and I understand and can appreciate it for what it is, but right now I had a battle brewing surrounding Ellie and a pixie queen and heaven knows what else—I needed to be levelheaded and ready for anything, and Tor needed to respect that.

The man in him would. I was sure of it.

Hoped, anyway.

Vampires are jealous beings with a streak of protection surrounding their possessions that was legend. And yes, the vampire in Tor saw me as his and his alone...so.

Sigh. I didn't need this on top of the Ellie situation. Or the pixie queen situation...or...

Yeah.

"We need to draw her out in the open and see what she wants. I need to, since I'm the one she seems fixated on and no one else has spied her," I said.

"Maggie, if she's dangerous..."

"We will handle it. All of us." I hushed Tor gently as his growling became more pronounced. I didn't like the way Nathara was eyeing him, knew she fed on the drama, and still held a torch for Tor despite being with Sven. I know she's get turned on by his posturing and when his fang punched out a little, I knew I had the right of it. Nathara was practically purring when she addressed him.

"Down, Tor. Maggie can take care of herself. But if you want to throw some of that concern my way, I'm sure I won't mind."

Sven flashed her a look that Nathara didn't notice—or chose not to. Ugh oh...this wasn't something we needed right now.

Clearing my throat, I made to continue but was interrupted by a light show and dire prediction from Madame Myna.

"Doom! Doom is coming to the one that holds the key. All is not as it seems. Treachery is afoot and an unlikely source will come to our aid even as one who is trusted betrays all. Things are changing, the team will see this transformation, and some will not handle it well. You cannot stop what is coming but must embrace the messenger. The body cannot be moved until the pieces of the puzzle are gathered and the key is put in the lock...or Ellie will be a soul lost forever in time." Madame faded away and her swirling, glowing smoke settled to darkness.

"Did anybody write that down? Dara, for heaven's sake...can't you get Madame to warn us when one of those prophecies is coming?" chided Bella. "I got some of it on my phone recorder app. Anyone else?"

"I wrote down most of what she said. I saw her lights begin to swirl and suspected she might speak," replied Dara, looking a bit hurt at Bella's harsh words. It wasn't like she could control Madame Myna. They had a symbiotic relationship at the best of times, but at the worst, Madame could be a prickly pain in the behind!

But her predictions were usually spot on.

"Jeez, talk about bad timing! Like we needed that on top of our already extremely full plate!" griped Serena.

What we need to do is come up with some kind of plan and incorporate it into our responsibilities to the antique show. Sometimes I wished we didn't have that hanging over our heads along with our monster-fighting duties.

"We need a plan. Tomorrow is another day of work, then we should probably try to decipher the rest of this map," I said, waving the paper in my hand. I'd retrieved it out of my bag and kept glancing at it while we discussed the other matters.

"About that," said Antoine, "I've looked at the next clue, and I think I know where we need to go."

"What? How did you figure it out?" I asked.

"Read it, Mags."

Flattening the piece of paper on my thigh, I glanced at puzzle number two and began to read.

"An illuminating place to start is where the old oak sings. Follow the trail to the urn where modesty doesn't count. Inside you'll find a package of aid. You'll need it when you reach the man covered in birds. At his feet is your reward...but you'll need six inches!"

"Oh, that's *really* illuminating," drawled Nathara.

"Actually, it is—for me anyway," said Antoine. "You see, living here for a long time as I did, I know this city better than any other. Therefore, I know where the tree in question is. And I know some of the rest of the clue."

"You do?"

"I do. And tomorrow when we wrap up our chores, we will gather there and see what we find."

"It's a date then!"

* * *

NOW WE JUST HAD TO GET THROUGH another long day of appraisals.

The next morning went by quickly and after a short lunch break, I found myself dragging my feet before returning to my tent. A good distraction came in the form of Tor who'd swooped me up as I passed his booth, twirling me in a circle, then planting a quick kiss on my lips that still managed to leave me breathless.

"Heading back to work?"

"I am. What are you up to?" I asked.

"Ugh, please. I've spent the better part of the morning going through old encyclopedias this woman and her pain-in-the-ass son brought in. He kept posturing and going on and on about how I was cheating them on price. Quite frankly, those old books don't fetch as much as some would assume. After the fifth box, I was ready to pull my hair out, but what do you think I found in the six and seventh box?" he asked.

"I have no idea." Tor, being the book expert, usually regaled me with tales such as this, and I always found it fascinating how something so abundant could mean pennies—or millions. Apparently, Tor found something amazing.

"Inside box six was half of a pristine set of the 11th editions of Encyclopedia Britannica. When I say pristine, I mean just off production mint condition."

"A few hundred dollars then? I'm not good at that kind of thing."

"Baby...those 11th editions of Encyclopedia Britannica came out in 1911. They are amazing! It was the first of its kind to not only include American and Canadian influences, but well over thirty women contributed articles for it. It's a masterpiece!"

"Holy cow. And let me guess, the second box had the rest?"

"A complete set. Can you believe it?"

"I bet you whipped your phone out and got clearance from my father to buy the lot, am I right?"

"Indeed. He was practically bubbling with joy when he heard my description. We gave the woman a very fair price, even her son couldn't complain."

"How much?" I asked, knowing it would be a hefty sum.

"Well, a good quality set usually runs around three thousand. But these? We're talking collector quality. We gave her a check for ten thousand dollars. I offered to consign them and have her wait until auction, but the son jumped in and agreed to the first offer. When I informed the woman she could possibly make more if she waited, she smiled, shook her head, and told me not to bother. 'Charles will go through it whether or not it's ten thousand or one hundred thousand. This will do.' Can you imagine?"

Unfortunately, I could. I'd come in contact with quite a few Charles's in my time appraising.

"What does my father think they'll go for?"

"Oh, easily upward of eighty thousand I would think."

Wow.

We did a bit more canoodling before I pulled away, begging off any more personal time. I had a booth to run.

"Maggie, be careful, OK? I know you are strong and capable, but you're also giving me grey hairs, and I'm too young for it...or so my mother says."

"Your mother? What do you mean?" I asked alarmed. Tor rarely mentions his family. What did his mother have to say about grey hairs and me? I didn't like where this was going!

"Nothing. It's nothing. Just...please don't go running off if that woman shows up. Get one of us...any one of us, please. Don't confront her alone."

"OK, I promise."

"Good. That's all I ask. Now be off with you before I pull you behind these bushes and have my way with you, woman!"

I returned to my tent to find a smallish line of humans, not a paranormal in sight. Good. It looks like my afternoon would be easy, and I'd be ready to take on this treasure hunt of sorts tonight with my group. I just hoped things didn't get crazy!

Yeah, right. When did they ever not?

CHAPTER 10

"*I*'m hungry and my feet hurt." Sydney hadn't dressed for a romp through the city park. That's where we found ourselves that evening after closing the appraisals down for the day. The rest of us brought a change of clothing and were in casual clothing and sneakers. Not Syd...she was teetering on stilettos in her business smart suit and even had her name tag on.

"You could have reminded me!" she grumped to no one in particular.

"It's too late for that now—you'll have to suffer," said Serena with a smirk. Those two had one heck of a bizarre relationship. Half the time they were inseparable, and the rest of the time they sparred like the weapons masters they were.

Seriously. Serena and Sydney dealt in all manner of swords, guns, knives, and other dangerous sharp and deadly objects. The only thing deadlier in their booth was the two of them, dressed to kill, and enchanting every man within fifty miles.

We didn't have far to go after work. Fairgrounds neighborhood was adjacent to the city park, and Esplanade Avenue led us directly into the main entrance...so we did what we'd done since arriving in New Orleans. We walked!

Once at the entrance we could hear the tree in question off to our right.

"Singing Tree indeed!" said Dara in delight.

"A local artist came up with the concept to place several windchimes hidden up in its branches, and it makes a lovely sound day and night," Antoine informed us.

We walked across the lawn heading toward the big pond and came to gather under the tree. The sun was low in the sky and cast shadows everywhere, making the moment a soothing respite from a busy day.

Looking down at a plaque at the base of the tree, I read the message and smiled. "Listen to this, 'Let the wind bring you a melody, a smile and a sense of peace and nature.' That's a nice sentiment, no?" I asked.

"Maybe if we had time to sit and contemplate nature, which we don't. Some of us have more important things to do," sniffed Nathara.

Grr.

"Well, Nathara, while you were busy being a bitch and poking at Maggie, I did that important thing. Or discovered part of it anyway," said Bella with a wicked gleam in her eye.

"Oh? And what is that?"

"Look! It was taped to the other side of the tree."

In Bella's hand was a large manilla envelope with the words 'Fortune Only' written across it with a black marker.

"Oh that's not too suspicious," grumbled Ellie.

Indeed.

"What's inside?" I asked.

"Huh," said Bella. "It's just a mini-Maglite flashlight."

"Oh a sense of humor on this one," chuckled Sven, albeit without nay humor.

"What do you mean?"

"The passage said, 'An illuminating place to start is where the old oak sings,' well...a flashlight can illuminate the way."

Groan.

"Oh that's cheesy! Whoever is doing this has a bad sense of humor."

"What's next? I need to keep moving or my feet will fall off," whined Sydney.

"Take off those infernal heels and walk barefoot then!" cried Serena.

"Ew, and step on something creepy crawly that I can't see in the dark? No, thanks."

Considering it wasn't dark enough yet for that to matter, I thought Sydney was overreacting a tad, but she put on her game face and trudged along behind us as we followed Antoine to our next destination.

A large cream-colored building loomed up ahead, and we made our way past the pond.

"What is that?" asked Dara.

"That is NOMA, the New Orleans Museum of Art. The urn in question is right out front."

"How can you be sure?" asked Ellie.

"It has naked men cavorting in a row carved on it. I would think 'the urn where modesty doesn't count' has something to do with that one."

"Sound good to me! Let's go stare at some naked carvings." Ellie didn't wait for us but whooshed off toward the building in the distance. Bella shrugged and began to jog after her in pursuit.

"I really hate these games," said Johnny, suddenly and heatedly. "I mean, if you want us to find something or do something is all this drama really necessary?"

"Relax, wolf breath. If someone showed up out of the blue with information on Ellie, we'd pounce and drill them without mercy," said Nathara. "What if this person has information but doesn't want involvement? Or has mild guilt in some small part they played but isn't the bad guy?"

"I'm sorry this is involving the lot of you," I said. "It's not fair and..."

"No! Do not apologize, Mags. You were there for me, and I for one, will always be there for you and Ellie." Johnny was earnest that I believe him...and I did. If there was one thing I knew about my gang of loonies, it was they were loyal to a fault.

Even Nathara.

"Except one of us might be plotting some kind of treachery," she said.

Or not.

"What do you mean?" asked Dara.

"Seriously? Did none of you hear Madame Myna? One of us is going to betray the group. At least that's what I took from her dire predictions."

I wondered when someone would bring that up.

"Perhaps it's a metaphor for something or it will be someone around us but not one of us directly," I said weakly. No one commented.

I didn't blame them.

"What on earth? What is that crazy elemental up to now?" Antoine commented, pointing to where Bella was doing her best to climb the risqué urn, Ellie hovering nearby offering her encouragement.

Even though the park officially closed at five, people could still be seen wandering around in the distance, and I was afraid Bella would draw a crowd—or a do-gooder would report a disturbance.

"There is no way she is going to make it up there and... well, in she goes! Now what?" I asked.

Bella heaved herself up and toppled into the urn which

must be empty, since her bum was sticking out of it, and I couldn't see her torso.

"What is she trying to do?"

"Got it!" We heard Bella's muffled voice before she'd righted herself and was grinning from ear to ear.

Jumping down from her perch on top of the urn, Bella turned and gave one of the naked figures a fond pat. "Good boy." Turning back to us, she held up a tiny shovel. "I used the Maglite to shine down in there and found this!"

"What are we supposed to do with that?" asked Tor.

"Dig a hole, son. Dig a hole." Antoine smiled and motioned for us to follow him as he jogged around the side of the massive museum and onto a wooded path.

We found ourselves in a wonderland of sculptures, from modern to classical and everything in between.

"What's with the blue dog?" asked Johnny.

"Obviously, it's to remind people to curb their were-wolves," said Nathara, barring her teeth.

"What about a memorial for burning witches? Perhaps there is a pile of sticks waiting for a bonfire and a dark witch we could use as kindling."

"I'd like to see you try."

"Children!" scolded Dara.

We wandered around seemingly going in a roundabout path since we were facing the museum once more, but then I noticed an odd sculpture which caused me to jump back.

"Eek. I think we've found our bird man!"

"That is hideous! Who calls this stuff art?" asked Bella.

"I believe the artist would consider this just that," said Antoine. He did indeed know his way around these land-marks because he made short work of the puzzle leading us to the last bit of it with ease.

"Well. What now?" I asked.

The statue was dark gray and portrayed a man standing

covered in birds. Like, they were embedded in his body and perched all over him like a bad nightmare. It was a creepy piece, although I'm sure some people found it pleasant.

The freaks.

"Now we dig. The last sentence told us how deep," said Antoine.

"Six inches," replied Tor, smiling.

"But where?" asked Ellie. "It could be anywhere!"

"I suspect at the bird man's feet. Or close enough to him since he's part of the puzzle."

Bella began to dig with gusto and soon had holes around the statue. I was worried we'd not be able to get everything put back without the grounds crew noticing someone had been digging, but then I thought, "so what?" Like, we weren't taking anything that belonged to the park, so no harm, no foul. I would just make sure Bella or whomever set things right before we departed.

"Hey, I found something!" Bella sat back on her haunches and pulled a little box out of the ground. It was small and square with a tiny clasp the only adornment.

"Quick! Open it, Bella!" cried Ellie.

"You got it." Bella finagled a few seconds with the clasp, then managed to lift it up and opened the box. Her cry of dismay warned us that whatever was inside would be disturbing to say the least. She'd gone pale and began to shake.

"Chuck! Oh my gosh! No. Someone killed Chuck and buried him under this statue!"

"How could someone be so cruel! Chuck was an innocent little pixie!" Ellie was sobbing and flew over to Bella's side. "Poor little guy."

"Let me see." Dara pushed her way forward and reached out to grab the box, carefully removing it from Bella's hands. "Give me some space."

After what seemed like hours with Dara murmuring to herself, she finally turned to Ellie and barked out an order. "Call Pandora here. Now. Chuck is still alive...barely, but there's a chance to save him."

Pandora? How? Why?

Ellie stilled and got a faraway look on her face. I knew she was trying to reach Pandora but when nothing much happened, she winked out of existence. Time was of the essence after all.

"Here, bring him into the light of this lamppost. Let examine him further." Dara was all business, her aversion to pixies set side as her cleric came out.

We gathered around the park bench where Dara sat, cradling a limp Chuck in her hands. Lifting him to eye level, she tried unsuccessfully to discern what was the cause of his weakened and lifeless state.

"Put him down, Dara. Put him on the bench and move away. All of you!"

Even before we'd noticed Ellie's return with Pandora in tow, we could all feel the electric pulse course through the clearing, then felt Pandora's arrival. Apparently, so could Chuck. He suddenly lifted his head and gave a pathetic mew.

That is until he began to growl and attempt to stand.

Pandora locked her eyes with mine and smiled grimly. "I don't like coincidence either, Maggie Fortune. Your sister is right. Too much of this stinks like someone is having fun at your expense. And it's going to end now!" Turing to face Dara, Dorie called out.

"Drop him, Dara! Hurry up and put him down!"

Pandora didn't wait for Dara to listen but used her magic to pick up the little pixie and fling him into the woods to our right.

"Dorie! Stop it! How could you do that to Chuck?" cried Ellie.

Pandora turned to face me again.

"When did you and Ellie speak? When did she tell you of my concerns regarding all these coincidences?"

"Kindred spirits...remember? She and I converse all the time telepathically, Maggie."

Pandora gave Ellie a solemn look.

"That's not Chuck, El. Well, it's not the Chuck we know and love. Ellie, he's a zombie! Or rather, he was made one with dark magic!"

A zombie pixie? For real? What could possibly happen next to top that one, I wondered.

CHAPTER 11

I didn't have to wonder very long.

"What was that noise?" whispered Nathara. She was clutching Sven, and never have I seen her more unnerved.

"It's coming from the pond," said Johnny who began to scent the air.

Pandora rushed over to us and examined Dara's hands. "He didn't bite you, right? Everything OK?"

"No, I'm fine. How could you tell he'd turned? How did he turn? He looked perfectly normal, if very weak," asked Dara.

"I can smell them. I... oh boy. What have you folks been up to that cause all this?" asked Pandora with a loud sigh.

"Cause all what?" I asked.

That's when the first gurgling growl sounded behind me, and upon turning, I found myself staring at what could only be described as a swamp monster zombie.

"Oh fudge!" (I'd like to point out I did not really say fudge.)

"It's a zombie!" cried Dara.

"It ain't Baby Snooks." Sorry. When I get nervous or go into one of our frequent monster-hunting capers, I suddenly recall lines from old Hollywood movies from the '40s and '50s. This time was no exception, and the line from The Ghost Breakers, Bob Hope's hilarious comedy, came to mind —and out of my mouth.

"This is horrible!" cried Bella, and again I had to stifle a giggle because now we are all inadvertently quoting the movie.

"It's worse than horrible because a zombie has no will of his own. You see them sometimes walking around blindly with dead eyes, following orders, not knowing what they do, not caring," I replied, rolling my lips to keep from laughing.

"You mean like Democrats?" deadpanned Tor with a wink in my direction. Obviously, he was well versed with the movie as I was saying the infamous line of Bob Hope's.

"What?!" cried Bella. Despite the calamitous situation, I finally let out a belly laugh and apologized. "Don't mind us. It's a quote from an old movie. I'm either losing my mind with fear or I'm exhausted."

"Quotes won't get us out of this situation, Mags. What do we do now? Look... there are more of them. They are coming out of the pond!"

"What did you do to call them?" asked Dorie. She was backing away and had her hands up, magic at the ready. "I won't be able to stop them if they've been spelled, just delay their forward progress."

"We didn't do anything other than dig Chuck up out of the ground."

"Up Chuck," snickered Sydney. I think she was reacting adversely to the zombie outbreak.

"We didn't call them. She did. Look over there!" Nathara pointed to a distant figure across the small pond. It was the old woman with milky white eyes. She had her hands above her hand and seemed to be chanting silently.

Changing the trajectory of her magic expulsion, Pandora slammed her spells into the woman, but it didn't seem to have any effect.

"She isn't really there. That's a fake image."

"That's some strong magic."

Even though the zombies were slow and dithered around mindlessly, a few had managed to reach us, and Serena and Sydney made quick work of them with their magical swords. Demon magic came in handy at times.

"There's too many. Look to our left. There are hundreds more coming from that direction!" said Johnny. Before we could react, he began to disrobe right down to his birthday suit. If we were supposed to look away, bad on us—the man was breathtaking. All sinew and Italian good looks. And what a nice...

"Ahem!"

"Tor! Um, what's he doing?"

"Zombies, in lore anyway, have no effect on werewolves. Johnny is going to shift."

And just like that, he did.

The next few minutes was a rush of fighting, with each of us making suggestions on how to handle the mindless wonders.

"Make sure you keep your distance and hit them with magic or an object like a large stick. They tend to..."

Bam! Splat!

"...explode on impact." I gave Nathara a dirty look when she came up to the zombie nearest me and thwacked him over the head with one of those chained posts used to keep people in lines like at a bank or amusement park.

"Thanks," I said.

"Don't mention it," she replied with a snarky smile.

The sheer number of zombies was astounding, but soon we had things down to a dull roar. Bella was using her earth magic to knock over an entire row of them, and we'd hack and slash until they were no more.

Pandora had taken off, giving chase to the shadow woman who'd tried to make her escape while we were otherwise occupied. I didn't know what she'd do if she caught up to her, considering the old women wasn't truly among us. But I'd worry about that later. Maybe Dorie knew something we didn't.

It wasn't until Chuck came tottering out of the bushes all fierce and frothing at the mouth that we realized the threat was over. Now we just had to dispatch our little friend to the other side.

I raised the thick stick I was holding, preparing to bring it down on the little pixie when Ellie cried out for me to stop.

"No, Mags! Not Chuck. Please! It's not his fault. We have to save him!"

"Ellie. He's a zombie. You can't turn a zombie back. Heck...I didn't know they existed, but even I know that has to be an impossible task."

"But it's Chuck. You wouldn't do that to me, would you? If I became a zombie?"

"Ellie, don't be silly. First of all, you..."

I watched in horror as two things happened. One, Ellie reached down and somehow managed to pick a snarling Chuck up in her hands. And two, Chuck, the little zombie beastie he was, opened his mouth wide and chomped down on Ellie's thumb, causing her to shriek.

How did she?

What...how...how did Chuck manage to bite a ghost?

None of that mattered now because just then, Ellie's eyes rolled to the back of her head, and she dropped to the ground like a stone.

Then she faded away.

"Ellie!"

My friends gathered around me as I nearly went out of my mind, running to the last place Ellie had been. There was no trace of her.

"Where did she go? Is she OK? Will she...will she become a zombie now?"

Chuck, for his part, was sitting down with a drowsy look of wonder upon his face. It was as if he wanted to know how he'd gotten here and what the heck was going on.

"Hang on a minute. Look at Chuck! He isn't a zombie anymore!"

"It was a spell," said Pandora, returning to join us once more. "And trickery. Who is behind this?"

I couldn't respond because I suddenly had visions filling my mind, causing me to fade into a similar situation as when I did a reading. In other words, I was no longer with my friends, but very much back in the presence of the Discordia in her realm. When I glanced over to where Ellie's body had lain before, I found my sister looking rather solid and weeping softly.

"Ellie!"

"Oh, Mags! What is happening? I feel so ill."

"Your sister is suffering the effects of having been bitten by a zombie. Had she remained in your world, she would have turned, then perished." Discordia rose from her dais and came to stand before me. I was surprised to see we were the same height. It wasn't that she appeared minuscule like the nyx she ruled, but I underestimated her size the first time I came to be here.

"You're behind this. Don't try to deny it."

"I am not."

"But your terms. You want the voodoo queen and wish to

have Ellie removed from your kingdom. Now here she is no longer a ghost..."

"Revenant."

"Revenant! Whatever! Now she looks all fleshed out. Like she's herself again. This had to be your doing."

"Yet it's not. I suspect the voodoo queen is trifling with us both, Magdalena Fortune. When Ygnarvish transformed, I sensed something was not quite right, and I've been watching. It was I who brought Ellie here...and you should be glad I did. Had I not?"

"Ygnarvish?"

"I believe you gave him the moniker Chuck."

I turned to Ellie. "Chuck is alive, El. Well, he was before I passed out or whatever I'm experiencing. He isn't a zombie anymore."

"He never was," stated Discordia. "A spell was put upon him. Once he infected Ellie, the magic passed to her. Even in ghost form, Ellie would have turned, and there would have been nothing anyone could have done to bring her back. Nothing except bring her to live here with me."

"No!"

I made to move on the pixie queen, but she brushed off my attempts to call up my magic.

"Don't waste my time, Maggie Fortune. Ellie will live here quite safely until you find the voodoo queen and bring her to me. Only she can turn your sister back. That...or you find the one who turned her into a revenant and reverse the dark magic which caused this tint upon my land. She won't survive if she returns to your world. I will keep her safe, as my guest, for however long it takes you. But you must find this vile woman and bring her to justice."

Even though I wanted to reject everything Discordia was saying, I couldn't help but notice the extreme transformation that had Ellie looking like her old self again. Surely she was here in her corporeal state. She was no longer a ghost.

"I'm so sorry, Mags. If I hadn't had picked Chuck up this might not have happened," said Ellie.

"But you did. And that woman knew it, or bet on it and won," said Discordia, gently.

"What if I don't believe you? What if I take my sister and leave this place? What then?" I asked.

"Then you are a fool gambling with your sister's life. I have no reason to lie, Maggie Fortune. Take Ellie away now and see what will become of her."

I couldn't do it. I couldn't risk Ellie.

Discordia saw my resolve melt away and knew she had us both where she wanted us. Now all I could do was trust her word—the word of a dark fae.

Wait a minute!

"Are you the queen of the danu as well?" I asked, thinking back to the dark fae we'd run across in Texas.

Discordia made a hissing sound and recoiled. "I have nothing to do with those vile creatures." Her eyes widened. "Eris! Is she the one behind this? Did she turn your sister into a revenant?"

"Is Eris the danu fae I ran across in Texas? If so, then not she per se... but her son, one Florin Vulpe. He turned Ellie and started this entire mess."

"Then Eris is behind it. She is the mastermind. Now I understand more, and the news brings me much unrest. I'd wondered how the voodoo queen came to such enhanced powers. Now I know. She is getting them from Eris."

"Are you related to her?" I asked, berating myself once more for being in the dark.

"No! There are many beings in the universe, Maggie. The nyx and the danu are not one and the same although they are lumped together by those who know nothing of such matters. We might be similar, but we are not the same. Find this voodoo queen, bring her to me, and I promise I will return Ellie to you unharmed. Trust me when I say she is in no safer place right now then here in Ninfea."

What choice did I have now? It was one of the most difficult things I'd ever had to do, but after a lengthy and weepy farewell, I left my sister behind to live among the nyx and returned to my world.

Alone.

CHAPTER 12

The next day was our first at Congo Square, the main antique troupe busy packing up shop and preparing to head out to our next locale, but we were to remain behind in search of this wretched voodoo queen.

Was I happy with the turn of events? No. Was everyone shocked when I came to and informed them Ellie would remain with the pixie queen for the foreseeable future? What do you think?

We had the bare minimum setup going on...just a circle of open booths, not a tent in sight. A small trickle of paranormals mingled with locals who didn't seem all that bothered by the odd-looking being that had gathered in their space.

The human contingency seemed to be making the most of the day with vendors selling enticing-smelling food stuffs and musicians doing their thing with many folks dancing and clapping along to their tunes. Blues in one section, some Ska across the park closer to the Louis Armstrong monument, ragtime, jazz, zydeco...everything blended and competed, but all was harmonious.

Harmony.

The opposite of discord.

My thoughts retuned to Ellie, and I didn't know how I'd manage with her in another realm and so far from me.

"Here comes another one, Mags," said Bella.

A fresh-faced shifter showed up holding some items that appeared to be family heirlooms.

"Hello. What have we here? Coins?"

"Yes. I have an eighteenth-century Spanish coin that I'd like evaluated."

I stared at the young man for a few seconds until I noticed him beginning to sweat.

"Are you going to tell me why you're really here?" I asked not unkindly.

"Um...OK...look. I have some runes. They belong to another pack, but I'm not supposed to have them. I just need to know if they are cursed or if they are what they appear to be. Simple ancient runes." A wolf pack then.

"May I ask why you wish to know this, and why you'd risk punishment having stolen goods?"

"They aren't really stolen. No! Not really. Please! The thing is...I'm betrothed to the girl whose family these runes come from. I need to know if they are cursed and if any of these bones belong..." The young man paused and blanched.

"He wants to know if any of these bones belong to one of his ancestors, Mags," said Bella, gently.

Oh. Egads.

I could see why he'd want to know something like that before accepting the girl's hand in marriage.

Shifters!

Crazy, the lot of them!

I removed my gloves and picked up the bones. Nothing. Not a trace of anything except a good kill, honoring the beast —rabbit, a deer, possibly a possum or two—with their sacrifice, but nothing more.

"Go marry your young lady. These are animal bones. *Real* animal bones...not, you know," I said, glancing around lest we be overheard.

"Oh! Thank you! Thank you! Here!" The young man handed me my fee and gathered up the items, stuffing them back into the pouch he brought them in. I wished all of my readings were so easy.

The day continued with similar appraisals. Nothing stood out. Nothing dramatic happened. That is until thirty minutes before we were supposed to wrap up for the evening.

I felt that same sensation of dread come upon me.

I quickly stood and began to peer around the square, certain I'd find the visage of the old woman staring back at me. But she wasn't there.

Instead, I began to walk around the area, taking in all the sights and sounds, trying to ascertain where the unease I felt was coming from. I told Bella to turn my sign over, letting everyone know I was closed. Then I took off.

I passed Tor doing another book appraisal, this time for a vampire female who was so super focused on my boyfriend I almost stopped to mark my territory. Not liking how it made me feel and trusting Tor had everything well in hand, I gave him a wink and moved on.

Johnny was faring no better being surrounded as he was by at least seven women, all various Breed, all wanting him to check out their wares. Furniture, I mean.

No, that's not what I mean.

Serena and Sydney were doing brisk business, as was Antoine. Dara was giving a palm reading to a group of giggling teenagers, and Sven had his head tight with a map collector—their cartography geek coming out in droves as they gushed over some small detail in the map laid out in front of them.

Nathara was at the table next to his, appraising some costume jewelry.

What was causing this disquiet?

"Maggie! How goes your show?"

Turning, I found the lamia, Dalila, walking toward me with a wide grin on her face.

"It looks like you're making a killing. I'm just glad the pixies haven't made an appearance." She'd whispered this last part so as not to be overheard in case any humans were close by.

"Yes. It's been a good day."

"And where is that lovely vampire? Antoine is it? Ah! There he is."

I didn't like her predatory stare and obvious desire to get her clutches into Antoine. But he was certainly old enough to fight his own battles, so I stayed out of it despite it rankling.

"If you don't mind, I think I will just go pay him a little visit."

I smiled politely but didn't say a word. Just as Dalila was about to turn, something in her eyes caught my attention. For just the briefest moment I saw them cloud over like a veil came down over her orbs.

A milky white veil.

Reaching my hand out to stop her, I pulled it back at the last minute, recalling Tor begging me not to take on any baddies alone. Instead, I sent a psychic message out to the one person I knew would hear it.

Within seconds, something so beyond the pale happened even I, with my frequent trips to the fantastical, was left speechless.

Pandora, in all her glory, showed up guns blazing. But instead of breaking out into a massive fight where assuredly some humans and even a few unknowing paranormals might get in the crossfire, she did something so outlandishly shocking I remained frozen in place.

No. Really. Pandora stopped time.

Everyone around me...heck, maybe all of New Orleans if not the world, was frozen in place. I don't know if she wanted me to witness this feat or if something happened which caused me to be frozen yet keeping my faculties had occurred, but I was able to watch despite my frozen state.

"Hey there, doll. What's the rush?"

To say Dalila was shocked was an understatement.

"What is this? Who are you?"

"That doesn't matter. What does matter is this. Dalila is it? Well, hon, I have a question for you, and I need an honest answer. What is it you most desire in this world?"

For a moment, I thought Dalila wouldn't answer, but then something transpired that would keep me up most nights, I'm sure. The young, healthy-looking woman began to shudder and shake, and her skin began to peel off her body. Before I knew what had happened, she'd morphed into a rather large and dangerous-looking snake.

Her clothing pooled in a puddle where her feet had been, and the little charm she'd worn the night of her risqué dance was a broken trinket on top. After all, a snake didn't need adornment nor the garments.

But it didn't stop there.

As if that transformation wasn't bad enough, Dalila went into another. Leaving me frazzled, I watched as Dalila changed into the old woman with the milky white eyes.

"I want my youth back."

Pandora smiled like she'd been expecting that answer all along. If I wasn't certain I believed Dorie to be a powerful demon before this moment, her commanding the goings-on now, her ability to will the voodoo queen—for what else could she possibly be—and compel her to answer her query, was astounding.

"Do you now? And what will you give me should I grant this wish—because I can, you know. I can give you eternal youth."

"At what price?" whispered Dalila.

"Your soul. I get your soul, hon."

Dalila threw her head back and laughed. I did not expect that and wondered if she had more than a few screws loose.

"What good is my soul if I am to have eternal life? Deal! Give me my youth and you can have my soul when I am no longer!"

Pandora drew out a nasty-looking dagger and ran it across her palm, then grasped onto Dalila's wrist, doing the same to hers. Joining their hands together, I watched as a flash of light snapped and popped, then Dorie drew her hand away. There was no cut. On either of them. Not a drop of blood either.

"You can't keep me here, you know," said Dalila. "I know what you are and how this works. Once I agree to your bargain, you can no longer harm me—that wouldn't be fair, now would it?"

"You're right. You are free to go. But heed my warning. My friends will hunt you down. They will find you, Dalila, and they will bring you to a swift and just end."

Laughing once more, the voodoo queen circled around Pandora and looked triumphant.

"I think not. You just gave me eternal life, you foolish demon. My, but you suck at this game, don't you? But go ahead and tell them to try their best to find me and bring me in to answer to these charges. I look forward to it."

Even as she spoke, I watch in astonishment as her features morphed once more, and Dalila, the youthful and stunning version, was once more standing in front of Dorie.

"Oh, sorry about your little friend. I hope it didn't pain you too much to have to end his life."

With that, Dalila threw her hands in the air and popped out of the square—where she wound up, and how she managed this feat remained a mystery for now.

The rush of everyone coming back from the fugue state was almost too much for my senses. You don't realize what quiet is until you've experienced the entire world being stopped cold.

"You OK?"

"Pandora! You let her get away! How could you when you know I need her to free Ellie."

"But I didn't let her get away, Maggie. You'll see," said Dorie with a jaunty smile.

"I'll see what?" I asked in frustration.

Tor, Antoine, then the rest of my people came quickly to stand around me and face Dorie.

"What was that? I felt something happen, but everything seems fine now," asked Nathara with a suspicious glance for Dorie.

"Pandora froze time. I could see what was happening, but I couldn't move."

"She what?" Serena, Sydney, and Bella began to hiss. Oh no! Not again. I could not deal with a demon war right now when I needed answers.

"Stop it. All of you. Listen, she was here. The voodoo queen. It's Dalila."

"What?" Tor whisked his head in my direction, worry written all over his features.

"Pandora made a bargain with her—eternal youth for her soul. Dalila accepted and I watched the contract—the magic sealing her fate, happen. But then Pandora let her get away."

Dorie rolled her eyes dramatically and popped the gum in her mouth.

"Such drama! I did not 'let her get away,' Maggie. I told you."

"How can you say that? I heard her. She said you sucked at this because you gave her eternal life for her soul, but now she can't be killed so you'll never get it. And you let her walk off!"

All eyes turned to Dorie who smiled like the cat who'd swallowed the canary.

"Maggie, Maggie, Maggie...there is no such thing as eternal life. Don't you get it? Everything has an expiration date. Even vampires. Even elementals. Oh sure...Dalila could theoretically live forever, but there are ways of doing her in —secret spells and weapons—that even eternal life can't escape from. I mean, you stake a vampire with silver and stick him in the sun. Eventually his body will give out and there is a moment in time where his awareness crosses into the veil and almost joins the soul once more, but...well."

"Well, what?" asked Antoine, looking shocked and something else...hopeful?

"Well, if that vampire had an arrangement, say with a demon of my caliber...that awareness could once again merge with the soul and the vampire would be no more...but the soul would go on to live another day in another life. Even on another plane of existence. It's the same for all immortals."

"You'll get her soul someday. Won't you?" asked Dara.

"You can bet on it and take that money to the bank, sister!"

CHAPTER 13

I'd like to say things went back to normal and we packed up and moved on to our next stop. But this was not the case.

While Dalila disappeared for the time being, we still had a few leftover zombies to deal with, and the marauding pixies hadn't let up. I'd finally called out in desperation to Discordia who'd deemed it in her best interest to beseech the few pixies to end their reign of terror and leave us be. After all, their true reason for being on a rampage was because their king, one King Ygnarvish, was now healed and basically back to normal. How normal that meant Chuck could be was still up to debate.

That he was king of the pixies?

None of us wanted to ask the obvious question. If Chuck was their king, did that mean he was married to Discordia? None of us could bring ourselves to ask. I mean...he was a tiny blue pixie that resembled the Disney character Stitch...only with a large nose and protruding lower teeth. And he has bushy eyebrows. And hair nose.

Discordia was a full-sized woman and...

Yeah. I wasn't going there.

She'd carried Chuck back to Ninfea and he conveyed to me, via Dorie, that he'd keep Ellie company, keep her spirits up, and protect her while she was his guest.

I couldn't ask for a better guardian than the pixie king!

After another two days of cleaning up the mess, we finally had New Orleans back to normal. Well, as normal as New Orleans could ever be anyway. We still had one more riddle to solve and this found us gathered, along with Dorie who'd decided to remain with us for the time being, at an ice cream shop in Mid City.

"OK, I don't know about you, but I am loving this spumoni. Angelo Brocato's is famous for it," said Bella, shoveling another huge spoonful into her mouth.

I don't know how she didn't get brain freeze!

"They've been here since 1905," said Antoine. "I used to come here all the time."

"I couldn't concentrate on niceties, however, not with Ellie stuck in the fae realm.

"Dorie, you said you didn't allow Dalila to escape, but we don't know where she is or what she'll do next. I can't get Ellie back without her. I can't concentrate on anything less until I do."

"I know exactly where Dalila is and who she's with," said Dorie smugly.

"What? How?" Everyone made so much noise with the quick response to question Dorie that we were drawing attention to ourselves form the other patrons and wait staff.

"Hush. Look at what you've done!" she chided.

"Dorie...please tell me what you're keeping from us."

"If you'd let me speak without interrupting, I'd tell you!" she said. "When Dalila transformed into the snake, she inadvertently left some of her snakeskin behind. After she ran off, I grabbed some and have it still. With it, I can find her, even if she goes off to another plane. Heck, I could find her even if I didn't have it...it would take me longer, but she sold me her soul Maggie! Trust me. I can find her anywhere."

Well...OK then.

"But what about knowing who she is with?"

"Hadn't you noticed the charm around her neck?"

"Um...yeah, sort of. I mean, I knew she'd dropped it when she morphed into that fiendish beast."

Dorie smirked, reaching into her purse and pulling out the broken necklace, the charm still dangling and sparkling in the shop's lighting.

"We agree coincidences are bogus. Have a gander at this charm. Does it ring any bells for you yet?"

My blood ran cold, and all sound left the room, but not because Dorie froze time. I managed to do it all by myself this time.

Dangling on the end of the broken necklace was a charm of a wee red fox.

Florin Vulpe.

Dalila was somehow connected to all this through Florin Vulpe—and that meant the dark fae, his mother, Eris. Again.

* * *

"How come I feel like no matter how many times we solve these puzzles others will follow?" I was maudlin and I knew it, but I missed Ellie something fierce and despite knowing she was being cared for by Chuck, it still hurt.

"Just read the passage, Maggie. What does it say again?" asked Tor kindly, his arm around my waist, offering support.

"It just says, 'finish the sweet treat and Angelo will give you a reward.' That's it. Nothing else."

Just then, a man approached our table with a small glass cup with a scoop of ice cream in it. He seemed dazed, and was definitely human, so we quickly assumed he was under a spell compelling him to approach our table.

"He's one of the guys in back making the ice cream," whispered Bella.

I took the offered treat with thanks, but the man just turned and walked away.

"I'm stuffed. Who is going to eat it?" I asked.

Johnny sighed and grabbed the bowl out of my hand and proceeded to polish off the ice cream with gusto.

Left in the bottom was a tiny key with a tag like you find attached to a safety deposit box. The tag was numbered on one side.

424

The other side had three words written on it...

Las Vegas baby!

I glanced around the table, watching the realization hit everyone at different times.

"We're supposed to be in Vegas in a few months!"

"Yeah, because Maggie's dad is a clueless wonder and booked us there in the middle of summer where the shade gets into the triple digits," said Nathara.

"I can't wait that long! I need to go now!"

"Maggie. We have to do this smart. We need help. We need to reach out to your superiors at The Order of Origin. This is getting out of hand, and we might have to call in some big guns," said Antoine.

"No! I can do this. We can do this. We don't need help from Delvin and the brass. Maybe I will speak with him, get his opinion. But nothing else. Where are we scheduled next?" I asked.

"Mobile, Little Rock, Oklahoma City. Then we have a weeklong break before we make our way out west. We arrive in Vegas in late June."

I looked around at my friends and couldn't help feeling a

swell of pride for our successes and knew we couldn't lose faith now. We were badass. A team like no other. If anyone could bring this guy in, this Florin Vulpe, grab Dalila in the process, and fix things so Ellie was back home, it was my team.

We might have had a setback of sorts losing Ellie. But now we had names. Now we had the tie-ins.

"We can do this."

"You know we can, Maggie!" said Tor, while everyone nodded in agreement.

"And you have me now. I'll be sticking with you guys for the time being. I mean, what could go wrong? It'll be great!" cried Pandora.

Bella beat Serena and Sydney to the hissing fits. But they followed suit shortly thereafter.

Oh, no.

"Yeah, and if we can survive fighting these baddies, get the answers we need, and rescue Ellie, meeting my mother in Vegas will be a piece of cake," mumbled Tor under his breath. Only I heard him loud and clear.

Wait. What?

Tor's *mother?* In Vegas?

Tor met my eyes and smiled. "And my sister too."

Help!

* * *

THANK YOU FOR READING! I hope you enjoyed this latest installment.

There is only ONE way I am ever going to attain world dominance and become a best-selling paranormal mystery and romance author. I need your reviews! Won't you please help me achieve my goals? Reviews mean *everything* to an author; it allows others who may not have heard of me yet take a chance on one of my tales. Amazon, Goodreads, and BookBub are just a few places you can leave them. I hope you consider taking the time to write one for me—and again, I thank you!

I hope you loved meeting Maggie, Ellie, and the rest of the characters. The next book in the Fortune-Telling Twins series, No Kilt About It, is coming soon! Maggie and the crew are heading to Las Vegas, and everyone is looking forward to the visit except Maggie. Why? That's where Tor's mother now lives, having moved there from Asheville, that's why. And the last thing our psychic witch wants is to meet the mother of the man she's involved with...especially since mommy dear is half vampire and has an imposing reputation as someone who has chewed up and spit out the last three of Tor's girlfriends. With the distraction of getting the answers needed to free Ellie from the fae realm, and a safety deposit box to find which might lead them to those answers, the last thing Maggie needs is Mommy Dearest breathing down her neck! Nobody likes vampire bites!

And if you enjoyed A Pocketful of Pixies you'll love reading about Maggie and Ellie's cousin, Lily Sweet, a naive dark witch who discovers her powers and reunites with a family she never knew while coming to terms with her topsy-turvy magical ability. Home Sweet Witch is Book 1 of The Lily Sweet Mysteries and is FREE on Kindle Unlimited!

"Excellent."

- Butterfly & Birch Reviews.

For a dose of steamy paranormal romance, check out Tarni Vanderzee's story...Lily's siren friend, in my new series, Secret Sirens. The first book is Siren Rise. It's a tale with romance, mystery and suspense that goes over Tarni's life from eighteen onwards as she tries to defy the conformity and misogyny among the sirens, live among humans, and seek out fame, fortune, and power. Enough power to overthrow those that rule the siren world. Only something gets in her way. An up-and-coming rock star named Logan MacDuff who has secrets of his own, the kind that might get Tarni into deep water...deeper than even she can withstand.

READ SIREN RISE here!

I'd appreciate your help in spreading the word, including telling friends and family. Reviews help readers find books! Please leave a review on your favorite book site.

You can also join my Facebook Group: Author Bettina M. Johnson's Team Wicked for exclusive giveaways and sneak peeks of future books—and just plain silliness!

SIGN UP FOR BETTINA M. JOHNSON'S NEWS-LETTER: http://eepurl.com/gZKo51

SOCIAL MEDIA LINKS

I write in my own style that may not be everyone's cup of tea —so if you enjoy my characters and humor, my plots, how the storyline is developing, etc. and are eagerly anticipating the next in the series, be aware that I am just as excited as you are—I've found someone who thinks my story ideas are neat! That is thrilling for any writer to know (or it should be). THANK YOU!

Visit my official website to receive updates, find out about special offers and new releases, or read my blog about writing and farm life - complete with photos - you might even catch me mowing my ten acres (seriously): http://www. bettinamjohnson.net

For more information or to contact me:
author@bettinamjohnson.net

For even more (if you just can't enough of me) follow my
Social Media Links

Mailing List - https://bit.ly/2BvQXmP
BookBub - https://bit.ly/2Epejwj
Goodreads - https://bit.ly/3aTejQW
Author Page - Amazon - https://amzn.to/3lj7L2L
Instagram - https://bit.ly/2QpZa01

TikTok - https://bit.ly/2PQa6Hg

MeWe - https://bit.ly/36A2RcM
Facebook - https://bit.ly/3gOaFZY
Twitter: https://bit.ly/3jahMgY
YouTube - https://bit.ly/2Stvy2X

ABOUT THE AUTHOR

I always knew I wanted to write. As a kid, way before the technology age had hit, I'd be stuck in the car with the folks as we drove from our home on Staten Island, NY, where I was born and raised, to our family property in the Catskill Mountains. To drive away boredom, I would sit, staring out the window, and create adventures of daring thieves riding horseback along the road, trying to escape the law. Other times I'd imagine a wild girl riding her unicorn into battle (I had a vivid imagination - we didn't have video games yet!).

As the years passed, I'd start writing a book, then stop, then start again only to let life get in the way, until one day I had an epiphany—a kick in the pants moment. If I waited any longer, all those wonderful characters in my head would never have their stories told, and that made me sad. So, I treated writing as my career. Once I started, it became apparent nothing would ever stop me again. YOU, dear reader, are stuck with me until I go off to that great library in the sky...or wherever writers go when they crumble to dust in front of their typewriters (or laptops...whatever)!

I live in the North Georgia mountains on what I like to call a farm, with my husband and almost adult kids, a Cairn Terrier, three cats, and fish. Occasionally other critters show up to keep things exciting.

BOOKS BY BETTINA M. JOHNSON

The Lily Sweet Mysteries:

Home Sweet Witch

Witch Way is Up?

How To Train Your Witch

Sweet Home Liliana

Witch Way Did He Go?

Revenge is Sweet, Witch

Witch and Peace

The Sweet Spell of Success

I Spell Trouble

Sweet Briar Witch

If It Spells Like a Witch (Coming Soon)

* * *

The Fortune-Telling Twins Mysteries:

A Tale of Two Sisters

Double Toil and Trouble

Fire and Earth, Sisters at Birth

Kindred Spirits

A Djinn and Tonic

A Werewolf in Sheep's Clothing

A Pocketful of Pixies

No Kilt About It (Coming Soon)

* * *

Secret Sirens:

Siren Rise

Siren Star

Siren Fall (Coming Soon)

Made in the USA
Monee, IL
30 October 2022

16852913R00072